FIREFLY

A NOVEL OF THE FAR FUTURE

FIREFLY

A Novel of the Far Future

by

Brian Stableford

The Borgo Press
An Imprint of Wildside Press

MMVII

CLASSICS OF FANTASTIC LITERATURE
Number One

Library of Congress CIP Data for the 1994 Edition:

Stableford, Brian M.
  Firefly : a novel of the far future / by Brian Stable-
ford.
  p. cm. — (Classics of fantastic literature ; no. 1)
"A Unicorn & Son Book."
  ISBN 0-89370-376-1 (hardcover). — ISBN 0-89370-
476-8 (pbk.)
  I. Title. II. Series.
PR6069.T17F57 1994   93-339
823'.914—dc20   CIP

REVISED EDITION

CONTENTS

DEDICATION

For Steve and Jo

PROLOGUE

Time is not simply a dimension measuring the passage of days and nights. Time is a property and a function of the minds of men. And because the human race is finite—merely a passing phase of an evolutionary procession—so too, in a sense, is Time. The present seems ever to be moving to the future, but one day there will come a time when it has run its course. It is, after all, only a sensory perception.

When that time comes, for Mankind there will be no more future. There will still be days and nights, but for the human race, Time will have stopped. There will be no more progress, no more hope for the future—only aging and dying.

The flow of time will become an erratic, arbitrary current, easily modified by interference with the mind.

Time will, by then, have exhausted the spirit which makes men build. Cities will decay. Dreams only half-realized will crumble into nothingness. Man will cease to live—he will only exist, in a meaningless, animal-like fashion.

But there are forces other than Time...and there will always be dreams.

ABOUT THE AUTHOR

BRIAN STABLEFORD was born in Yorkshire in 1948. He taught at the University of Reading for several years, but is now a full-time writer. He has written many science fiction and fantasy novels, including *The Empire of Fear*, *The Werewolves of London*, *Year Zero*, *The Curse of the oral Bride* and *The Stones of Camelot*. Collections of his short stories include *Sexual Chemistry: Sardonic Tales of the Genetic Revolution*, *Designer Genes: Tales of the Biotech Revolution*, and *Sheena and Other Gothic Tales*. He has written numerous non-fiction books, including *Scientific Romance in Britain, 1890-1950*, *Glorious Perversity: The Decline and Fall of Literary Decadence* and *Science Fact and Science Fiction: An Encyclopedia*. He has contributed hundreds of biographical and critical entries to reference books, including both editions of *The Encyclopedia of Science Fiction* and several editions of the library guide *Anatomy of Wonder*. He has also translated numerous novels from the French language, including several by the feuilletonist Paul Féval.

PART ONE

UNDER TIME'S SPELL

I.

"THE RED WOLF"

Dewy sunlight barely filtered through the heavy clouds that moved ponderously across the sky. Fine rain descended in uneven sheets, but we were already completely drenched, and we ignored it. Our black mare trudged along with a miserable gait, which suggested that she was hauling the whole world behind her rather than an old wagon and two men.

The man who sat beside me was my brother, John. He was hardly more than a boy. He wore a large, thick fur coat buttoned tightly about his neck, which widened his slim shoulders to impressive but unconvincing dimensions. His legs were protected by sodden leather trousers, which must have clung like a second skin by now, leaden and abrasive if he tried to move. He didn't move. He sat very still. His head was bare, and rivulets of water ran down his face, so that pools accumulated in the corners of his eyes. Water dripped unsteadily from his pointed chin onto his knees.

Clutched between his delicate hands was the stock of a crossbow, elegant and powerful, whose gross size gave the impression that it would require stronger arms than its owner's to wind back the string with the clumsy cross-key. On his back was a quiver full of bolts. So far as I was aware, he had never been called upon to make serious use of the weapon, and to judge by what I had seen of his practicing, it was, perhaps, as well. But he hardly ever laid the weapon down, as though he thought his life to be perennially under some mysterious threat. He was not a coward or a madman, but he thought in strange ways.

11

His eyes clung to the ill-defined strip of bare earth that served as a road. Once there had been stone there, but the even surface had accumulated a thick coat of mud and dust, which had hardened into a hard carapace. Grass grew wherever it could, and clumps of the springy sphagnum moss that covered the nearby hills were beginning to encroach from either side. Carts and caravans rarely passed this way these days, and the road would eventually devolve into a pathway etched only by hoofmarks and footprints.

Far away, I could see a yellow light, which I hoped was shelter and a chance to get dry. John had not yet seen it, and I did not trouble to point it out. When he was like this, he did not listen. While he sat so still his head was occupied with words and ideas. He was constantly reflecting on tales he had heard of a man who had said that he could walk through time. We were following now in what we thought to be his footsteps. Which is not to say that I, personally, was in any way interested in such a man, or even in such fantasies. But we had no family, save for each other, and no friends either. Wherever John went, I would follow. Wherever he wanted to go, I'd take him. I'd looked after him since he was a child, and though he was grown now, I still fancied that he needed a certain amount of looking after.

The yellow light drew closer and closer, and when the black mare, whose name was Darling, noticed it, her tread became a little more enthusiastic.

It was an inn called "The Red Wolf." It was old, but possessed a solidity which promised much warmth and comfort within. We dismounted, and I left John to lead Darling round the back in search of a stable, while I inquired as to our chances of staying for a while.

The huge door creaked noisily as I shoved it open and slid round it without opening it far enough to let the cold wind blow into the room.

It was gloriously hot inside. Smoke from numerous pipes swirled gently into the eddying air, making patterns in many shades of blue and grey. There were four long tables in the room, one of them listing badly because of a broken leg propped up by an inadequate block of wood. Along the tables was arranged a miscellany of old and middle-aged men—all farmers by the look of them—and the occasional hawk-faced woman who was unmistakably not a farmer's wife. Some of them turned to stare at me, but most continued talking in heavy murmurs in between sips of dark beer, without even a glance in my direction.

At the far end of the large room was a crackling, spitting fire, in front of which sat a greasy-haired, round-faced woman of the type which does not age but merely suggests antiquity. Her eyes were fixed on me, flicking up and down to assess my nature and the contents of my wallet.

I threaded my way between the close-set tables without disturbing any of the sitting men, and addressed the woman.

"You own this house?"

"I'm its mistress, aye. I'm Queen. And you?"

"My name is Matthew. I have a brother named John, who is trying to find accommodation for our horse and wagon."

"There's a stable," she said, "but no feed."

"He'll find something in the wagon," I assured her.

"And where be you travelling to?"

"South." I gestured vaguely with an arm whose sleeve was already steaming. "We have no proper destination. We travel." By that, she probably took us for gypsies, which would at least persuade her that our wagon wasn't worth looting. In point of fact, it wasn't.

John came in, less careful of the draught than I had been, and some of those nearest the door grumbled. He ignored them, with his characteristic lack of tact, and came to join me.

"My brother John," I introduced him.

"I call myself the Firefly," he added. It was an annoying affectation of his.

"Why?" she asked. Everybody did.

"Because I reject this torpid world and cast a light of my own. We want a room for the night. Our horse is in the stable, and I've fed him from our own provisions."

She had begun to laugh, but returned to seriousness as his speech continued into its second, more prosaic half.

"Four pieces for two rooms. Two for one," she said carefully. I gave her two pieces.

13

"And one for the horse," she added, although I had been careful to give her no indication that my pocket contained more than the two pieces. I handed over another.

"I'd like a word with you, mistress," said John.

She looked at him, surprised. I shrugged, and moved off sideways toward the fire, rejoicing in the fierce heat which pained my face and hands. It was some seconds before I moved to a more reasonable and comfortable distance.

Meanwhile, John's words, thought spoken in a low tone, drifted across to me. "I've heard you called a seeress," said John.

That was news to me. We'd certainly never been this way before. But John talked to a lot of people. Possibly one had mentioned Queen of "The Red Wolf."

"Well?" she asked, warily. I looked round, and saw her eyes darting to the nearest of her customers. But the man either had not heard or did not care. He was talking to the man by his side about the weather.

"I've heard some of what you say," John continued.

"What's it to you?" she demanded. "It'll cost you if you want your fortune told."

"I'm not interested in fortunes," he replied scornfully. "Only in strange stories. They might resemble others that I've heard. I believe you got them from a man that I know, and I'd like to know where he is now."

She thought for a moment. "You shouldn't talk that way to one with the sight," she said, glaring coldly. He remained completely unimpressed. When he was sure of his ground, he was practically unshakable. "Things you don't understand," she went on, "aren't all lies."

"I'm not interested in lies either," said John, which was a good deal more diplomatic than some things he might have said. I reflected that he might be learning at last. "I'd like it if you just told me where the man went," he said patiently.

"Away," she replied evasively. "If rejecting this world means that you want his, then you're as mad as he was. He was always looking over his shoulder. Always afraid. But he talked all right. All the time. Yes, I use his stories to frighten *them*," she indicated her customers, "And why not? If I didn't see it, I know who did. And I gave him enough for it,

14

didn't I?" She stopped suddenly. "Who is he?" she asked. "Tell me that and I'll tell you which way he went."

"He was a man from another world," said John. His eyes ducked and dodged. "A long way from here. Didn't he tell you about travelling through time? Didn't he boast that he could? I'm sure he did because from what I know about him, he wasn't a man to let a boasting chance escape him. This world is dead, as you must see. Old and decaying. But he can go other ways. He can go back to the days when our cities covered the world. He can go wherever he likes—to times when there was purpose, and fortunes to be sought. I want to find him. I want him to take me there."

"And what if I told you he went back where he came from?" she said bitterly. "Back into the past, where you can't reach him?"

"Did he?" asked John. There was a hint of terror in his voice. This was a thing which he feared greatly.

"No, but he would've if there were a word of truth in the trash he talked. Why would he stay here if where he came from was so fine? He went west, into the barren lands. Deader than the rest of the world, if you ask me. Why would he do that, hey? With all those fine cities to go to? You're chasing a dream, child. A fairy story.

"He said he was looking for the future, but wouldn't walk to it. I told him—begged him—to stay here and share the future with me. He ignored me. A little while, and then gone—that's *his* way." Her lip curled slightly, as though there was a bad taste in her mouth. "He left me for the empty west. Left me with all his crazy ravings and idiot's stories. Left me to play seeress with his words. Nightmares too, he left me."

She talked too much, I decided. A fine pair, they must have made. "He left me with dreams, as well," said John, and moved over to my side, by the fire.

"Westward," he said, briefly.

"You know her?" I asked.

"I heard about her."

I laughed quietly.

"What's the matter?"

15

"Why do you go through all that?" I asked him. "What must she think of you, making ridiculous speeches about rejecting this world, and being left with great dreams by men who walk through time? Can't you see that she thinks this man is nothing but the prince of all liars? He talked her into bed with his fancy tales, and then went on to someone else. And you made her tongue run away with her—she'll hate herself for that, and you too. Why, John? You don't have to tell them all the crazy story. What sense is there in it?"

He looked at me with an expression which had been growing on his face for several years now. It was calculated pity. An "I-can't-help-you-if-you-won't-be-helped" look.

"You're dead," he accused. "Part of this whole rotten mess. Do I *have* to be ashamed of my reasons? Haven't *you* any reason for living?"

"Not a one," I told him. "And the sooner you find out that yours are illusions, the sooner you can settle down to an ordinary human existence."

He refused to say anything more; just sat and stared into the fire, wriggling in his wet clothes.

"We'd better go to bed," I said. "Let the clothes dry by themselves."

He shrugged sulkily, and I went to ask Queen to show us to our room.

II.

THE SUN

And so we went westward, at first over more or less verdant hills, and then into barren lands, left desolate and dead by over-exploitation and bad usage centuries before. We passed through a number of small villages, huddled round the rough road and sticking greedily to whatever pieces of arable land they could find. They were always cluttered with rubbish and infested by myriad flies, whose ceaseless buzzing annoyed us when we stopped in such places to eat or ask questions. We did not care to sleep in such places, unless the weather was particularly bad. It rarely was—the storm that raged the night we spent at "The Red Wolf" was the last rain we saw for some considerable time.

Wherever we inquired about the man in whom John was so passionately interested, we got much the same answer:

"Aargh....you arsk Anna 'bout 'im. Left 'er wi' child 'e did. Rode orf one mornin' before fust light. Weepin' in the street she wor, when she fund out. On 'er knees in the dust. Ya, straight west. Way the road goes, isn'it? On'y desert that way, though...."

And so we came to the desert. It was not a hot, sandy desert, such as they are reputed to have in the far south, but a wilderness of rock and dust—grey and iron red. It was the decayed remains of a city that had stretched a hundred and forty miles or more.

We were never troubled much by the desolation except when the sun was really high on cloudless days. It was on

17

one such day, with the afternoon just beginning, that we saw the second sun.

Darling was picking her way carefully round the cracks in the brittle, parched stone. The road was very bad here, despite the fact that it was unused—or perhaps because of it. The heat haze, reflecting the ruddy streaks in the ground, was making my head spin a little. I ignored the bright spark on the horizon for some time after it made its initial appearance. John said nothing, although I'm sure he saw it at the same time I did.

It wasn't until we got a good deal closer, and could make out the whole shape of the thing, that we began to take an interest.

There was a burning sphere about a yard in diameter suspended—without any visible support—between two metal structures like pylons. The air between the tips of the towers, which were swollen and bulbous, shimmered like a heat haze, except that the field was horizontal and the direction indeterminate.

"What on earth is that?" I asked John.

"A lighthouse?"

"Surely not in the middle of a desert. What keeps the light burning? Why does the fireball hang there, without a stem or wires?"

"How do I know?" he replied testily.

"It looks like a relic of your fabulous past," I commented, with a certain irony. "Surely there's no man on Earth today who could build a thing like that. Although no man of any age would want a lighthouse in a desert."

All the while we were growing closer. We could now see that the towers were set on a huge cylindrical base of stone. Beside the platform was a squat, square building with iron-barred windows and a door of solid metal.

"Built to last, at any rate," I said. "Perhaps the whole city fell down around it."

John was showing real curiosity now. Undoubtedly, this strange edifice *was* a remnant of his lost past. But what its purpose was—or had ever been—I could only guess.

A man came out of the squat building, and stood in the roadway, his arms folded across his chest, waiting for us to draw up alongside him.

As we did so, I nodded my head to him and said "Hello."

He nodded in reply, smiling slightly. He was small, and stood in a slanting fashion, as if one leg were a little shorter than the other, although I hadn't noticed a limp when he had emerged from the building.

John was looking upwards, shielding his eyes from the brilliant glare and the blast of heat which emanated from the globe of fire.

"What is this?" I asked the man.

"The Sun," he replied, and added "I am the Sun."

John returned his attention to the slanting man.

"Is it yours?" he asked.

The man beamed. "All mine," he assured us. "It is a fragment of the Sun"—he pointed up into the southwestern sky, so that we should be sure which sun he meant—"which I have captured and made one with me. The father gave it to me, so that I should know my identity."

I raised my eyebrows in slight bewilderment. It seemed obvious to me that the man was suffering from the heat of his baby sun.

But John was listening in all seriousness.

"Who built it? What holds it there, between the towers?"

The small man looked at us suspiciously. "Who are you?" he inquired.

"Brothers," replied John. "This is Matthew, and my own given name is John. But I take for myself the name of Firefly because I reject this world and cast my own light."

The Sun, as he seemed to style himself, laughed. It was a calm, ordinary laugh without a hint of hysteria or madness.

"Take care, Firefly, that your wings are not burned by this device which entrances you so," he scoffed. "Your feeble light is to mine as a shadow to the night! Burn the memory of me into your insect brain! Look at *my* light, with eyes unshielded! You can still see the blaze through closed eyelids. If you stare at it, it will blister your eyeballs and blind yourself forever. And yet *you* say that you cast your own light!"

John, taken aback, paused to think this over. In the meantime, I noticed that the lock on the iron door was broken, and that there had been writing both on the door and on the pylons, but that time had long ago erased its meaning.

"How long have you lived here?" I asked him.

"Forever," he said, as though it should have been perfectly obvious. "Ever since the father brought me here."

It was the second time he had said "the father" instead of "my father," but the dialects in these parts were highly variable, and I dismissed it as a figure of speech.

John was trying to look directly at the incandescent sphere. I shook him. "Don't be a fool. He's right...you'll blind yourself."

"There's nothing *in* there," he said wonderingly. "It's just fire. Pure fire."

"It's something sucked up from the ground," I said, "and discharged from both towers. Whatever's burning is deep beneath that concrete base."

"But it just hangs there," he protested.

The Sun—the small man, that is—watched us, smiling, apparently flattered by the attention we were paying to his alter ego.

Darling was beginning to sweat heavily under the fierce light, and I was not a little discomfited myself.

"We must bid you goodbye," I said to the man, who promptly stepped out of our way, nodding courteously.

The black mare moved on thankfully, and I turned back to watch the man return to his house.

John had returned his gaze to the road ahead, and seemed to be deep in thought.

"Did you notice?" he said.

"Notice what?"

"One of the pylons—the one nearest the hut. It was broken at the base."

"No," I replied, "I hadn't noticed."

"One day," said John, "that tower will collapse."

"I doubt it," I said. "It hadn't much weight to support, and it looked strong enough to me."

"Nevertheless," he predicted, "it will fall."

"You're just jealous," I said. I realized that he had actually been hurt by the Sun's reference to his careless choice of phrase in describing the reasons for his second name.

"My light may be pale," muttered John, as though speaking to a third person, "but it does not burn with such a consuming passion that I need worry about its destroying me."

I looked at him wryly. "I wonder," I said.

III.

SHADOWS

As the weeks went by, we emerged from the desert, traveled through the great dark forest of Holmchapel and—still heading due west—passed into the furthest of the western lands, the Vales of Stardene. Beyond this there was only the Singing Sea. I knew nothing of the lands that were now to the north, but the southern mountains—which the local people referred to as the Mountains of Misty Mourning, although they had other names elsewhere—were clearly visible on all except the dullest of days, when cloud and fog would cloak them completely. At its zenith, the sun hung over a giant crag known as the Peak of Sorrows.

We had no difficulty in finding out which way the man who walked through time had turned. He was a man who clung to other men's—and women's—memories. At almost every inn or roadside hostel where we stayed the night there was someone who had heard of him, or actually seen him.

Our passage through the Vales was slow. I was afraid for the health of my wallet, and we were forced to take work—picking fruit, usually, although we also had occasion to grind knives, mend roofs, and even put poor old Darling to the plough.

Every delay irritated John to the point where we spent long hours quarreling and sulking like a pair of babes. Time wasted meant, for him, all the more chance that the man who walked through time might disappear, like a will-o'-the-wisp, into the future or past. Or lose himself someplace on Earth where we could not find him.

He was headed south now, of that we were sure. I would have liked to go on a short way, to the shores of the Singing Sea, for the sake of idle curiosity. But even to mention the idea would have driven John into a fury, and I allowed him to choose our route at all times, except when I deemed it necessary to take work. In truth, my wallet was far from empty at any time, except when we first arrived in Stardene, but I dared not let that make me complacent. Soon, I had no doubt, we would be up in the mountains. where there would be no chance to make up the opportunities we missed now.

Despite our delays, our quarry did not gain on us. We had a mission—we knew where we were going. He, it seemed, did not—or if he did, he left no traces of it in the tales which lingered after him. He stopped at whim, and started again without any apparent pattern. I knew that we must surely catch him before the end of summer, no matter how many days we "wasted" in labouring for coin. If, that is, we were allowed to catch him at all. All he had to do in order to escape was to close his mouth. But why should he?

As we began to climb the foothills, still a great way distant from the austere mountain peaks, the days settled into their midsummer rut: the succession of short nights and long, hot hours of bright daylight. The sun was welcome at first, but its everpresence began to pall with remarkable rapidity. It sapped our sweat, and our energy with it. Darling toiled ever more slowly, perpetually weary and unwilling to work. I had not the heart to urge her, for I knew exactly how she must feel. John, of course, was as impatient and irritable as ever, but it was too hot to argue.

As we trudged the rock-strewn ascending trail, we saw a small figure far away in front of us. I could not make out what sort of a man he might be, at first, and he seemed quite oblivious to us, although we were clearly visible and probably the only moving object for miles around. We overhauled him slowly, and eventually he heard the noise of our cart-wheels crunching the loose stone of the road. He stopped immediately, for a rest he seemed to need badly, and watched us as we approached and drew level. I reined in, and looked at him closely.

He was a member of the Brotherhood of the Afterman: a small, bespectacled man with wizened, smiling features, which were unnaturally flushed and running with sweat. The heat had brought such color to his cheeks and forehead that he seemed to be slowly cooking. Yet he smiled cheerfully, as if it were the way his face was set.

"We have room, if you'd like to ride," I said.

"I would like that," he confessed, "but your horse is pleading with me to refuse." The mare was, indeed, regarding the little man with what seemed remarkably like distaste. I reflected that the way ahead was mostly uphill.

"Very well," I said, "we'll lighten her burden. It wouldn't do for her to sweat all her weight away. Young John here's a featherweight, and you're not large yourself. It's my own mass that's causing her all her troubles. So I'll take a turn at walking while John guides her."

John seemed completely apathetic to the whole exchange. The little man barely hesitated. He was obviously far too uncomfortable to waste time with polite refusals of proffered help. He clambered up via the front wheel, and I gave him a hand by which to pull himself up on to the seat beside me. Then I swung myself over him and jumped lightly to the ground. He glanced back at John, who came forward from the wagon to take the reins. He smiled even more broadly, and nodded to the boy, then returned his attention to me.

"I'm Brother Álvaro," he said. "Or Father Álvaro, if you prefer it." I offered him my hand, and he took it. "Matthew," I said. "Father to none but brother to the skinny one. He's John, the Firefly."

"And why's that?" Álvaro asked John.

"Because I go my own way," John replied, a fraction listlessly, "and need no one else's light to guide me."

"Just someone else's horse to carry you," I muttered, under my breath. "Being a firefly on a day like this seems to be a particularly pointless pursuit," I said out loud, as they both turned questioning eyes upon me because of my inaudible comment. I didn't want John to begin one of his long monologues on the uselessness of my existence in particular and modern existence in general, although I could hardly hope to stop him.

I went forward to pat Darling's big black head, and she turned towards me with an appealing look in her eye.

"We've been treating her too harshly," I called back to John. "We must stop as soon as we find shade." She really did look a little desperate, and I was seriously concerned. Sometimes John's impatience caused me to forget that Darling had to be considered too. After all, apart from the fact that a sick horse would delay us a great deal longer than a rest once every hour or so, I loved the old girl.

"I cast the light of reason," muttered John, more to himself than to his new companion. It might have been a rebellion against my silent wanting, or it might have been that he had guessed the substance of my earlier remark.

Brother Álvaro remained suitably solemn.

"We're following a man who can walk through time," said John in a somewhat brighter voice, as we moved off in search of shade. "Do you know anything about him?"

Álvaro's surprise was evident in the tone of his voice, though his words did not express it. "A strange way to spend your days," he said, avoiding the question.

"Have you heard of such a man?" persisted John. I *had* told him about politeness, but he'd never taken the slightest notice.

"I believe I have. But I don't know where you might find such a man."

John lapsed into silence again.

"What are you looking for?" Álvaro asked him. "An adventure in time? Knowledge? An escape?" I reflected that he seemed to take all three notions far too seriously. I glanced back at him, slightly puzzled. He was still smiling complacently.

"I want happiness," said John.

"And what is happiness?" the priest demanded.

"I don't know," replied John, with no hint of humor. "I haven't found it yet. To be content with my life, I suppose, as my amiable brother Matthew is content with his. To have reached a destination or crossed a barrier. To be at ease. Not to be ceaselessly at odds with the world. To know that what exists is what I need to feed me. That's what's the matter with this time, this world. It isn't *right*. There's always a gap between myself and life. Friction, all the time."

"And you believe that to walk through time will solve all your problems, take away all your cares?" said the little man, as though he *knew* that it was not the right answer.

"To the Golden Age," replied John, his voice taking on an edge in the face of implied argument. "The age of Man's greatness. Before the human race began to die. I want to go back to the days when we owned the stars, when great cities stood in the places that are rust-deserts today. That's *my* time. That's what I want."

Álvaro shook his head, and mopped his brow. He removed his spectacles, and began to polish them attentively. The heat had apparently damped out all his enthusiasm for the debate, and John, for the moment, would say nothing more while his assertion remained unchallenged.

I returned the whole of my attention to the road, looking out for trees or spires of rock, which might offer us shadow in which to rest and recover.

There was something moving, not very far ahead. I saw it once, and then it was obscured again as the trail dipped. As we came to the next rise, I looked for the movement again, and watched for several minutes before the figure became recognizable as a youth of some twenty years capering about on top of a group of sun-parched slabs of rock beside the road. He seemed to be driving himself furiously, gyrating and leaping up and down, picking up small pebbles and hurling them high into the air. But all the time, his eyes remained fixed on the rock beneath his feet.

My first thought was that he was stamping to death a snake that had attempted to bite him and failed. Then I considered the possibility that he was suffering some kind of a fit. I turned back to Álvaro and John, who were also watching the dancing figure.

"What do you make of that?" I asked.

"I hardly know," replied the little priest. "Why don't we ask him?"

"We don't want to be delayed," said John suddenly, in his inimitably tiresome fashion. "It wouldn't do to become involved with a madman."

Apparently oblivious to our existence, the youth continued hopping, twitching and stamping.

The road deteriorated on the downslope which led to the outcrop, and Darling had to select her way down with painstaking care, avoiding runnels and holes. John sat back on the seat, letting me find her a way, guiding her by the bridle. He watched apprehensively as the youth leapt off the rock, ran up to within ten paces of me, then stumbled and fell headlong.

I moved forward to help him, but he was up before I reached him. There was a gash stretching from the center of his forehead to his right ear. He mopped blood away with a grimy sleeve and silently faced us. I moved forward again, but he shied away, as though suddenly ashamed of his clumsiness. The sudden movement apparently reminded him of another injury because he stopped, stood on his right leg, and moved his left knee between his hands. He looked pained and a little sheepish.

"Well," he said, "what's the matter?"

I shook my head and spread my palms to indicate that I meant him neither harm nor offense, and said, "I was only coming to help you."

He put down his left leg gingerly, and plucked at his lip with long fingernails. "Who are you?" he demanded, ungraciously.

"We're travelling west," I said. "My name is Matthew. We were wondering..." I paused, unsure how to choose my words.

He wasn't listening to my slowly forming inquiry.

"You cast a shadow!" he accused.

"So do you," I pointed out, somewhat taken aback. "What about it?"

"Do you like it?" he wanted to know. I paused before answering, to study him more closely. He was about John's age, with John's slim build. But unlike John, who was a rather personable youth, this one was decidedly ugly. His mouth was large and bulbous, and his skin stained with pockmarks. His eyes were sharp and lizard-like.

"I don't mind it," I replied finally. "There's not a great deal that I can do about it." I smiled. "One might almost say that I'm quite attached to it."

"I love my shadow," said the youth.

This time I was completely startled. I had been inwardly amused at my silly joke, but the young man's seriousness jolted the humor out of me.

"Is that so?" I remarked. without levity.

"I've heard of people who were afraid of their shadows," the youth went on. "Lots of them. Murdered in suspicious circumstances, they were. No apparent cause of death. A friend of mine said they'd had the evil eye put on them. Now who do you think might do a thing like that? *Look out!*"

He pointed at the ground between my feet. I leapt like a frightened rabbit. By the time I came to earth again, I was furious with myself for having been caught like that.

"It was reaching for you," said the youth. "You have to be careful. Don't give it half a chance."

"My shadow...," I began testily, but was not allowed to continue.

"Won't happen to me," he interrupted loudly. "My shadow and me, we get along just fine. I love my shadow, I do. You ought to make peace with yours. Nearly got you just then. Lucky I warned you, you are. What if I hadn't been here, hey?"

I could hear laughter behind me as Álvaro and John rejoiced in my annoyed bewilderment. Even Darling whinnied in a distinctly sarcastic tone.

"You want to be careful," continued the irrepressible youth. "It's with you wherever you go. It's always looking at you with those invisible eyes. At night, it'll haunt you and you can't see it. You just have to sit there, shivering with fear. And in the daytime, it'll call its friends to help mock you.

"It might be planning to kill you. This minute. Right now. It can hear me, and it'll be afraid that, from now on, you'll be on your guard. It won't like that. It'll bide its time until you relax just enough for it to slip through and strangle you. Don't go to sleep tonight. Not without making your peace with your shadow."

"You're mad," I said hopelessly. "You're completely mad."

He ignored me. "I love *my* shadow," he said proudly. "I don't have to be afraid. We help each other. We talk to each other. We dance together."

"So *that* was what you were doing...," I began again.

"We go everywhere together," he continued, without deigning to recognize that I had tried to interrupt. "We'll always be together, for ever and ever."

I gave up, turned away and returned to Darling, deciding that there was no further point in staying here.

We trudged on, in our search for shade.

"Now there," I heard Álvaro say to John, "was a man completely at ease with his world. A truly happy man."

"Yes," agreed John, and added, "As long as the sun shines."

IV.

CONQUESTS

"Man conquered the stars," said John.

"Did he?" said Álvaro. "I don't believe so."

It was a tired argument by now, but Álvaro seemed content to talk and talk and talk. And John knew no better than to carry on trying to convince him—or to convince himself. I didn't join in—not any more. I just drove the wagon.

The hot spell was over now, mercifully, and we were making slow but sure progress up into the hills. We had progressed from the farmlands of the lower valleys to the tree zone, where human habitation was far less evident. The roads were long and winding and usually alarmingly precipitous. I often had the impression that we were driving mile after mile to get absolutely nowhere, because for every up there was a down, for every left bend a right bend.

"It's true," insisted John, waving his arm in a long arc above his head, tracing a line across the evening sky. "Once, every star—every single one—belonged to *us*. To our race...to this planet. Until we gave them up, and came home to rot."

Álvaro laughed softly, and John glowered at the little man's persistent refusal to be impressed.

"We reached so few," he said quietly. "So very, very few. We went, and we planted our flags, and we said our brave words. We looked around, and everything we saw seemed to be within our grasp. After all, the stars are so tiny, up there in the sky. And no one can even *see* their tiny satellite worlds. But we never could grasp them—because they aren't just tiny lights in *our* sky. They exist. They have identities of their own, and we couldn't force them to take on the identities *we* wanted, just for our own purposes."

"They never belonged to us and never could have. It was all a dream, my friend, like your own dreams, brought on by pride and false sight. You must see that a man is not the beall and end-all of existence. He is only one part of a continuum—a link in a chain that leads, we know not how far, to the final evolutionary achievement. Perhaps there will be no final achievement, and the chain will go on forever. But in either case, man is only a passing phase. The Brotherhood of the Afterman has adopted, as one of its tasks, the mission of teaching men to appreciate their own position in the scheme of things. The Brotherhood does not teach human glory, but human humility and human understanding. We have no gods, whether graven images or visions of vanity. We have only our small place, our true existence. We teach not the futile triumph of Man, but the eventual succession of the Afterman. Our race must die, and there *will* be life after death. It will not be *our* life, even though it be the life of our descendants. It will be a new way of life...the Afterman.

"Do you know how men pushed their way out to the stars? They took a tiny piece of this world—the air, the substance, the quality of our own Earth—and they wrapped it up in a steel coffin. Then they pushed the coffin all the way to the nearest star. Then they pushed it all the way back again, and *said* they had conquered the stars. Without the small fragment of Earth enclosed in that box with them, all those men would have died. They could not live in space, nor on the star worlds. Only on Earth.

"To *conquer*, don't you see, you have to make something *yours*. You have to make it into a part of you— something that you can control and direct.

"We could never have done that. Only Earth, and nothing else, belonged to us. We need it too much, you see, like the early life needed the sea. Even after life emerged from the ocean on to the land, the land wasn't *conquered*. The lungfish didn't conquer the land, and neither did the amphibians. The reptiles were the conquerors, because they were the first to develop the cleidoic egg, which freed them from dependence on their ancestral ocean home. There's a big difference, John, between going somewhere and belonging there. Man can't conquer the stars, because he can never free himself from the planet of his birth. When a man goes to the star worlds, he has to take Earth with him. The great conquests, John—all of them—will be the prerogative of something beyond what we are. The only purpose which Mankind *can* serve is to give birth to the Afterman."

John had long ago lapsed into deep sulkiness. He often did, when no one would see his point of view, or admit to the rationality of his arguments. He couldn't argue with a man as clever and as articulate as Father Álvaro. John, for all his affected maturity and self-confidence, knew so very little, while Álvaro knew so much, and had had twenty years or more longer to prepare his case. I would not have said that Álvaro was a very wise man, but he was a determined man who was perfectly clear about what he believed, and what he was doing with his life, and why.

To fill in the embarrassing silence, and to cover up somewhat for John's sulkiness, I asked Álvaro, "What do you suppose they *felt*, the men who flew iron boxes to the stars? What do you think they thought of themselves when they landed on new worlds of new suns?"

"Why," said Álvaro, as if it were obvious, "they felt like conquerors—what else?"

And isn't that enough? I wondered silently. Isn't that all the boy wants, really? Do we, so old and so clever, really have to challenge his dreams? But I didn't say so. To say so would only have hurt John even more, and it was not for me to criticize Álvaro.

"Well, Firefly," I said, trying to jolt him out of his black mood, "shall we stop for the night here? The sun has set, and Darling's eyes are not so good as they once were. We don't need shelter on a night like this."

"The sun is only just behind the mountain," he said. "We'll have a few minutes more, once we're a little further along the road. And there's twilight too. A mile or two, Matthew, that's all."

I shrugged. One day, on roads such as these, poor old Darling would finally give up and say to herself, "No further, not one step." I felt perennially guilty about placing my brother's whim before my horse's welfare, simply because he complained the louder.

"I am the Firefly," said John to himself, but loudly enough for Álvaro to hear and understand. It was his credo. "I am the Firefly," he continued, "because the sun's light gives life to everything on Earth, and I have life beyond that possessed by all others, and thus cast a light of my own. I do not need the daily circle of the sun. I reject its futile light and go my own way. This world is dead, but other men are content to live and breathe as the cells of the corpse. But not for me. I want to go back to the time when life was like my life—when it meant something. I follow a man who has the secret. Man has forfeited his future, but there is life in his past, and this man can take me there, or show me the way. I *will not* die. I am the Firefly."

"That is a proud boast," commented Álvaro. "And I hope that you do not regret it. A name—especially a chosen name—must be worn, and worn forever. Even if there is a time when you no longer wish to be the Firefly, you will never forget that name. Be careful, John."

"I can live up to my name, *Father*," said John, "if you can live up to yours."

"We are all fathers of the Afterman," countered Álvaro. "For life comes only from life. As your ancestors were apes, and before that insect-eaters, and before that reptiles, and before that amphibians, and before that fish, and so on back to the primeval astraea, so there will come from ourselves the Afterman. And from him, who knows? *We* cannot know, for even if we were to see the Afterman, we could not understand him."

"I don't care about your Afterman," retorted John. "If there's no future for Mankind, there's none for me. I will go into the past."

"The past," repeated the bespectacled man. "The glorious past, which so obsesses you. Go then, if you can find a way. But remember this: if you do commit yourself so utterly to struggle and ambition and power, then you deny yourself the contentment which is here, now, in this world. Perhaps it is not your kind of happiness, if you insist. But for many,

many men it is near enough theirs. It is the nearest the race has ever come. Don't be blinded by cities and stars, John. They're only symbols. They were always false, although the people who built them would never admit to their foolishness. We *are* a better people now. More advanced, more mature. Nearer to death, of course, but that is the path time takes. Man, in this day, has learned to live with himself, and that is something which you will not find in the past.

"You're a rebel, you say. You feel pressures that no one else seems to feel. But what is your answer? To run to where *everyone* feels these same pressures. Can that relieve them? Can that even make them more bearable? I pity you, my friend, because you are not taken by a glorious ambition, as you think, but afflicted by a disease."

A cruel man, Álvaro was, although he would never recognize it in himself. John had been lulled into a sense of dull anger by the ceaseless. smooth, cutting flow of Álvaro's words. He reacted now that the little man's monologue was finally done.

"You! You preach to me of the sin of pride, the disease of ambition. But what is your Brotherhood, Father Álvaro, but an institution which has taken it upon itself to determine the destiny of Mankind? You say that you recognize no illusions of vanity...no gods. Yet you want to play God yourself. You prepare for the Afterman. You teach the triumph of the Afterman. What gives *you* the right to determine the future?"

"We have no right," admitted Álvaro. "You are correct, in a way. We take a great deal upon ourselves. We act where perhaps we should only wait. But we do not do so because of pride. We do not say that we are The Chosen, who will lead Mankind to its destiny. We make no gods in our own image. We do not play God. We only play what we conceive to be the role of man. Your accusation has a hint of justice. This we know, and of this we are ashamed. We act for our beliefs, and it is impossible to know that there is no vanity in such an action. Vanity, after all, is such an easy and self-concealing sin. But we do as we think we must, John. We do not deny that we may be proven wrong. We retain that humility, at least."

More silence.

We had not seen the sun again, despite John's confident assertion, and I finally reined in without bothering to consult him for a second time. I had leapt from the wagon and was busy unhitching Darling before he had even contemplated a protest, so he left it unvoiced.

As we settled down for the night, I said to Álvaro, perhaps a little late in the day, "It had always seemed to me that the lungfish could conquer the land. It breathed air, not water."

He shook his head in long-suffering patronization. "No, Matthew. A fish that breathes air is still a fish. Just as an ape without hair is only an ape who thinks himself more handsome. The lungfishes came out of the water to breathe the air. They contrived to walk on land and hunt food there. They could live through long, waterless summers. But they still needed water in order to make new lungfishes. They were not the whole bridge between sea and land—only a small part of it—the beginning. But their sons and the sons of their sons were moved by chance and selection, diversified and reclassified. And eventually, at the end of a long road with many blind branches, the reptiles came.

"There is one main line, you see. One line that goes from the bottom of the tree to the topmost heights. But no one is ever sure which line it is. It's not a straight line. That line leads to man, but it will go *through* man. Because man is the topmost branch *now* does not imply that he is the limit of the tree's aspirations. He grows still, he changes still. There will be more and higher branches. We cannot tell how high the tree might grow, or whether it will ever stop."

"And what will be the form of your Afterman?"

"I don't know! I will not see him. Time seems to fly, you see, but in reality it is very slow. I fear that someday it may stop altogether. That day, perhaps, will be the day of the Afterman. I'll die long before then."

John was moving, and I went to say goodnight. But he was already asleep. Dreaming, no doubt, of a new morning. Of a meeting and a journey. He was curled up within his blankets, like a fetus.

"He sleeps like a child," I said to Álvaro.

The little man shook his head as though to disagree. But he did not trouble to explain himself.

V.

OLD MOON

As if our way into the mountains were not already winding enough, the man who walked through time now began to change direction as often as we asked his way. The mountain villages were few, and scattered with no pattern around the slopes, connected by crude pathways that hardly ever saw wheeled transport. He seemed to be intent on visiting every village. Obviously he was in no hurry, but so tiresome and difficult were the ways we had to take in order to follow him that we nearly despaired of ever catching him.

Here, I think, he might well have found out that we were following him. His route was so circuitous, and news traveled so fast between the hamlets, that news of our quest could easily have reached one of his ports of call before he did.

But gradually we moved ever closer to the lonely western peaks. Since we had left the main cart-road for the rambling ridge-paths and goat-tracks of more recent formation, the distances between habitations were so difficult to traverse that the night was often well advanced before we were able to find shelter. We did not like to sleep out in the open so high up because the bitter cold wind which often blew out from the peaks could turn our sleep to agony. We began to appreciate having the Brother with us at this time—people knew him, or at least his fellows, and were pleased to offer us food and shelter at little or no cost. John hinted that it would be interesting to know what service the Brotherhood was likely to render them in return for their solicitude, but he was often churlish with respect to the doings and thoughts of Father Álvaro, and he was judiciously ignored.

On one occasion, we rode for a near-solid fourteen exasperating hours when wheels persistently jammed in cracks, and the wagon had to be constantly loaded and unloaded to allow Darling and myself the chance to haul it clear. It had been dark for an hour when we heard the voices on the night wind, but a wondrously large and bright full moon hung heavily atop the Peak of Sorrows.

The voices appeared to be chanting—a fact that bothered neither myself or my brother, but which seemed to agitate Álvaro.

"Be careful, Matthew," he warned. There was trepidation obvious in his voice. For a man so confident and habitually calm, it bespoke an ominous strangeness.

"What's the matter?" I demanded, reining in.

"It might be something with which we might not want to be involved," hedged Álvaro.

"But what?"

Finally, he confessed. "I don't know. I'm in unfamiliar territory. We're further west now than I've traveled before. I'm afraid I've allowed my liking for your company to carry me out of my way a fraction. But that's not important. These isolated villages often have weird ways. Don't judge every hamlet by what you see in one. Mountain people keep themselves to themselves, and their habits too."

"But they're only singing," I protested.

Darling began to move forward again, of her own volition. She must have had enough of argument these last few days to last her until eternity.

We stopped again in the shadow of a large-boled tree, looking down into the village. The people, some sixty or seventy, I guessed, were gathered in a large circular space on a mound, set back from the road and without the perimeter of the houses. The chant contained many archaic and unknown words, and had a very deceptive rhythm. I could follow it for three or four words at a time, but always got lost before picking up the real sense or content of the thing.

After several minutes, I was able to make out that the singers were mocking or insulting some object or person.

"What shall we do?" I asked.

"I'm tired," said John. "Let's go on. They're harmless."

"They seem to be all right," agreed Álvaro. "But watch your step if you talk to anyone."

John lifted his massive crossbow from between his feet and laid it across his knee. He placed a bolt in the gullet of the device, but did not wind back the string.

We moved forward, creaking ostentatiously.

Not everyone chanted all the time. There were some six or seven ringleaders and twenty or so devoted followers who just stood around watching, laughing softly at some especially choice insult every now and again, and adding their voices to the odd chorus here and there.

We stopped on the road, looking up at the mound some twenty yards or so distant from us. I stood up to see better, and both John and Álvaro craned their necks. We didn't see or hear the man who came up behind us until he cleared his throat politely.

"Hello," he said.

I nearly jumped clear off the wagon.

It was John who replied. "Ah," he said, as though we'd been expecting company. "We'd like to find beds for the night, if that's possible."

"Well," said the other, who was standing in our moonshadow, and therefore difficult to make out clearly. "I don't know as I can help ye, it bein' fuller moon. Ye come at a bad time, ye see. Sendin' day an' all. Maybe later, some'un can fix ye up."

"I take it," said John, rushing in where Álvaro had warned us not to tread, "that *this* is sending day?" His slender arm indicated the mound and its ritual.

"Aye."

"What are they chanting about?" John asked, with his customary direct approach to a subject.

"Old moon, of course."

"Why? What has the moon done?"

I tried to follow the other man's expression, but it was too dark. I sat down, and let the moonlight strike his face, and he shied away. He was a nondescript fellow of medium height, with coarse features and a casual voice. When he replied, though, the voice was calm enough to soothe my worries. No one, it seemed, wished us any harm.

"Old moon brings darkness, my friend. We're trying to destroy him, an' so bring about the eternal end o' night."

"No, no," corrected Álvaro, before he could stop himself by remembering his own advice, "it is the setting of the sun that causes nightfall." I could feel his quick embarrassment as he remembered asking us to be careful of *our* tongues.

"Ye speak nonsense, sir," the villager returned gently. "Old sun cannot cause the night, for old sun is never here o' night. Old moon rides 'pon the night and hence must be the cause. It's surely obvious to a wise 'un such as yerself."

Álvaro was reluctant to let such absurdity pass unanswered—he was always a man full of his own rightness—but he was doubtful of the wisdom of continuing, and so hesitated.

John, on the other hand, was intrigued, and not in the least reluctant. "But doesn't the moon often appear during the day? What of the days when the moon rises before the sun and lingers in the sky after dawn, and those when it appears before sunset?"

"Ah! Old sun is clever, ye see. He gathers his strength while old moon commands o' night, and can often 'whelm him in surprise attack. T'other way, alas, is also true, an' old moon, often as not, wins an easy victory in th' later daylight."

John was obviously puzzled by the reference to attack and victory. "But the sun and moon do not fight for possession of the sky," he said. "They are merely passive bodies revealed and hidden by the turning of the world about its middle."

Álvaro, beside me, caught his breath and held it. John might just have spoken heresy.

"Don't be silly," said the mountain man. "If that were th' case, the days and nights would all be th' same length an' th' same kind."

That shut John up. He hadn't anticipated that angle. He knew that there was a flaw somewhere in the argument, but for the moment he was at a loss to understand exactly where.

However, he was stubborn. "But aren't there nights when the moon never shines at all?" he tried.

"Ah!" said the other again, as though we'd just reached the crux of the whole matter. "That's our doing. When old moon is at his largest and most powerful, an' threatens to bring the forever-night, we send out a warrior to help old sun. And the next night, old moon is not so big an' strong. Our warrior, fresh an' hearty, from Mockingbird Mountain, is pinning him back an' winning the fight. For a fiveday an' more, our warrior always forces old moon further an' further into hiding, till o' last, old moon takes refuge elsewhere. We pray then—oh, how we pray, 'cause we know that when old sun comes back he might ha' returned home forever. But never quite. Our warrior's never managed to pull off the final blow. I don't know where old moon goes or whatever he does, but it must surely be foul cleverness. Always he come back out, slowly an' sneakin'. Weak, no doubt, from having kilt a mountain man—we're strong, ye see. But old sun can never quite finish the job for us. Old moon always gets back his stren'th, and we have to go through the whole thing agin.

"But someday, friends, someday—mark me now—there will be a man with a *mighty* soul. A man who's lived so long his soul is like granite, and lived so strong that his soul is a hero's soul. *Then* we'll see old moon run. He'll be beaten one day. Mark me. And then 'll come the forever-day. And ye'll remember me then, won't ye?"

John, still not defeated, although somewhat deflated, was reduced to inquiry. "And how is this warrior sent to his work?" he wanted to know.

The man pointed to the edge of the mound, where a great stone wheel was balanced, and I perceived for the first time a stone runway descending the gentle slope to a gully which seemed to be shaped just neatly to receive the wheel's curvature.

"We lay him in th' trough, and the whole village gathers round to heave the stone over the lip. It smashes him to a smear, and his spirit's freed from his body. It floats up'ards into the sky. to do battle for us and for the world." The man pointed dramatically at the moon as he finished his explanation.

41

John had nothing more to say, for once. I pursed my lips, and I could almost feel Álvaro saying to himself that we'd been warned. I think he was afraid that one of us might wind up in the trough.

But that was not the way. They wouldn't have trusted us to fight their battle for them. Nobody takes such liberties when they have to fight for the future of the world. It was only a few minutes more before the sacrifice put in an appearance. He walked out of the village, flanked by a holy guard. They did not need to drag him. He was an old man, but frail. He seemed to have lived long, all right, but I doubted that he had "lived strong." Apparently, so did he. His step faltered, and his eyes were wide. There was not a vestige of self-confidence in his pitiful frame. His body moved mechanically in the grip of fear.

He passed within three or four yards of the wagon, and as he did so, he looked at us. There was pleading in his eyes, and I think he wanted to scream for help. But he did not— either because he did not dare, or because he was ashamed of his wish.

"Move," I said to John, who held the reins loosely in his hand. He sat as if petrified, watching the great stone wheel. I kicked him on the ankle, seized the reins, and gave Darling a solid flip on the ear. She whickered, and moved off. I refused to look anywhere but at the road ahead.

John half rose to his feet, and murmured something inarticulate. I sat down hard, grabbing him by the scruff of the neck and forcing him down as I did so. But I couldn't stop him craning his neck and staring.

There was a solid thud from a long way behind us, and a sound of seventy voices bidding a friend a fond farewell.

Old moon seemed to be smiling.

VI.

THE STATUE GOD

"We could have helped him," said John.

"There was nothing we could do," I replied coldly.

It was the next morning. We had spent the previous night out in the open, and had not been spared the chill of the wind. My reasoning, of course, was unassailable, but even I felt a little repelled by the totality of its conclusion. *Nothing.* Nothing at all. But guilt is not always responsible.

"And you," John reproached the Father. "You, a Brother of the Afterman. Could you sit silently by and watch such a thing happen with such ease? Or was it *merely* a man, and thus of no concern?"

"He didn't watch," I said accusingly. "Only you did."

"No, he didn't watch. He turned his back, like you. But what difference does it make whether your eyes were pointed in or out?" He sounded bitter and angry. "All right, *I watched* with my eyes, although both of you wanted to pretend that you couldn't see. You're hypocrites. We were *there*. It *did* happen."

"There was nothing we could do," I insisted doggedly.

"Never mind you," said John. "You always were a coward. But *you*, Brother. You're the man who has answers. You're the man who lives in the best of all possible worlds, who knows that we're all contented, all happy, that strife and suffering are over and done with. Well?"

"Sometimes," replied the priest, and he, too, sounded bitter, although it was a different kind of bitterness, "one has to stand silent. It does not mean that I condone what we saw.

It does not even mean that I was afraid to act. Your brother is not a coward. He did what he did because he had reason. Because there was no good to be done. I did what I did because I had to. I do not like to fear the consequences of my actions. I like to act—against reason if I must. Even when there is nothing material to be gained, I like to be right, when I can be. Having acted always rests better in the memory than having stood by. But men must not be subject to each other's laws and morals. The edict of the Brotherhood, by which I am bound, says clearly that the way of life which men adopt is *theirs*, and is not for our interference. They may be helped, if they ask for help, but they must not be forced to fit another man's mold. They must not be changed because another man deems them to have contravened some imaginary law, or principle of humanity.

"The Brotherhood of the Afterman preaches above *all* else *tolerance*. And we must tolerate not only the poor and the weak, the hated and the denied, but also the rich and the strong, the haters and the denying. It does not taste right—not to me. But if it tastes right to *them*, if it is their way, then they cannot be charged with any crime."

"Why?" moaned John. "Just tell my *why?*"

"Because my duty—the duty of the Brotherhood—lies to the Afterman, not to man alone. Our law is to bring forth the Afterman, and to guide or use men only to serve that end. In all else, we are bound to leave men alone, unless they ask for our help. And then we can offer only certain kinds of self-help. Never intervention. We cannot offer the kind of help which that poor man might have cried out for.

"Our time is over, John. Remember that. We cannot have the right to change other men into what we would like them to be. The whole race of man has already proved to be inadequate to his own aims. There is nothing to be gained by preaching new ways of life, except the renaissance of the ceaseless strife which such action prompted in the past. *My* effort is directed in preparing the way for a new race. Out of man—perhaps such men as these mountain people—will come the Afterman, delivered by our beliefs, created out of our tolerance. As soon as we become intolerant, and begin forcing other men into our own mold, or *any* mold, there is strife. And out of strife can only come death. Man must not be allowed to destroy himself, John. And he nearly has, on many occasions. Because in destroying himself, he would destroy the Afterman. Mankind must fade quietly away, John, giving birth before he is completely gone."

"I don't understand you," complained John. "I don't think you understand all that yourself. When you're accused, or questioned, you just talk and talk and talk. You know your catch-phrases by heart, but when you string them all together, there's nothing but froth. There aren't any answers there, are there? You're just running away with eloquence. I *know* you're wrong, philosophy or no philosophy, because what you've *done* is wrong."

"I don't know," said the little man, wiping his spectacles on his sleeve. "I can't say. Is there a *right* to which we must compare ourselves, as you say, or seem to say? I think not. There is no cosmic rule, no divine ordinance. There is only choice. I have chosen. I abide by my choice. There is nothing more."

"I will never make a choice like that," John declared. Nor I, I wanted to add. But I wasn't sure that I hadn't made such a choice already.

It was about noon when we saw the statue. Curiosity, and a certain tiredness because of the previous night, led me to rein in and dismount in order to investigate this strange decoration of the lonely mountain road. Alvaro also got down to stretch his legs, but John remained up on the wagon, affecting total disinterest.

The statue was fashioned from a mixture of gray and brown clays. At first, I took the colors to be a pattern of some sort, or at least arranged for visual effect, but they gave the appearance, on closer inspection, of having been applied quite haphazardly. It was as though the sculptor had not troubled to examine the nature of the clay he had used, but simply collected all he could and molded it as it came to hand.

The figure was a grotesque parody of a human form. Slightly shorter than myself, its head was abnormally large, giving it the semblance of a giant child. Its eyes were malformed. Where the eyeballs should have been there were only shallow pits with the nasal ridge in between. The depressions were scarred, as though by the scraping of a fingernail, perhaps to suggest eyelashes. I decided that the eyes might be closed, although the figure stood up and could not be supposed to be asleep.

It was bald, with a rounded skull showing no trace of knitted bone-seams. Its mouth was twisted and its ears shapeless masses of ill-adhering clay—they looked as if they might have been added as a late afterthought. It was nude, and the skin around its groin was quite smooth. There was no trace of pubic hair or any genital or excretory organ.

I was inclined to dismiss it as a rather poor statue. but it had some intriguing qualities.

"What do you make of it?" I asked Álvaro.

"It pleased someone to make it," he replied, "or he would not have chosen to display it by the roadside."

I looked around at the surrounding slopes.

"I can't see any sign of a village," I commented.

"The country is so folded and twisted that we could be within a mile or less," he pointed out. "Look how little of the road we can actually *see*, both in front and behind."

There was ample truth in that. The mountainous country could be very confusing to travelers who were unfamiliar with its peculiarities. One could lose one's landmarks with ludicrous ease. It would have been perilously simple to lose our direction continually but for the presence of the road, which presumably would not waste too much mileage in getting to where it was going.

"I think there are more up ahead," called John, pointing. There were definitely more shapes of gray and brown, but they seemed to be recumbent, not upstanding as this one was.

We remounted the wagon, and moved on. About a hundred yards beyond the first, we found the remnants of a second statue, which had been felled by some unknown hand and shattered. From what we could see, it seemed that this statue had been, in all respects, similar to the first.

Over the next half mile. we passed seven more statues. Two were whole, the rest were in varying states of destruction. They differed in height and attitude. Some stood, some knelt, some ran. Their arms, too, were in different positions...extended, upraised, folded. But they were one and all eyeless—or nearly so—and sexless. They seemed, in quantity, to be the representation of something inhuman and slightly fearsome. One had been an enigma, nine suggested that someone was obsessed.

Eventually we came to a wooden hut surrounded by pine trees. It was small but pleasantly constructed. Outside the door a huge man sat, shaping a great mass of clay into a statue such as we had seen on the road. He worked silently, and his hands moved slowly. But the emergence of the characteristic figure was steady and clear.

For a moment or so we sat in line at the head of the wagon, watching him without really knowing what to do or say. The giant, who must have been eight feet tall, or within an inch of it, was pale and comparatively thin. He either failed to detect our presence, or was so completely indifferent that he was prepared to ignore us without even a cursory glance.

At last curiosity prevailed, and I dismounted. John followed me this time, helping Álvaro down after him. We all three approached the seated man.

"Good morning," I ventured.

The giant did not look up. "Monster," he said.

"Monster? Is that your name, or do you mean me?"

The giant continued smoothing the head of his creation into a reasonable approximation of a chinned sphere.

"Did you place the statues by the roadside?" I asked, though it was something of a silly question.

"Statues." The giant spat on the ground. "Men."

"Yes, I noticed they were men," I said. "Some of them have fallen over. Perhaps the wind." He remained impassive. "They're broken," I added.

"Dead," he commented, with a slight shrug of his shoulders, as if to indicate that it was the way of the world, and it was not worth his while to shed tears about it.

"It's a pity," I said, struggling for conversation.

"Men die," said the giant, who was obviously a fatalist. He didn't waste words much, either.

"You'll wear out your tongue," I commented. "You don't mean to tell me that all those statues were once alive?"

The giant at last looked up. His face was childlike, and bore an ingenuous expression of surprise.

"Men live," he stated.

"Statues don't," I retorted.

He sniffed. "Men do," he repeated, as if that were the end of it. He returned to his work.

I turned helplessly to John and Álvaro. John obviously thought that I had discovered another madman, and was enjoying the exchange. Álvaro hung back, watching as though he were also waiting. Determined not to make a fool of myself again, as I had over the shadow affair, I turned back to the big man.

"Why do you sit here making men?" I asked politely.

"God," replied the giant.

"You're God? Who told you that?"

The giant extended a finger. "Ring."

On the finger, third of the left hand, was a metal ring with a large colorless jewel set in it. The giant twisted his hand so that John could stare right into the stone.

"Be careful," warned Álvaro, as John leaned forward to peer closely at the gem. I glanced at the little man, and returned my attention to John just in time to catch him as he fell over.

"Don't look at the stone," said Álvaro, coming forward and placing his tiny hand over the giant's huge fist. The giant took his hand away, glanced at the ring himself without any apparent effect, and went back to shaping the nose of his statue.

John sagged in my arms, and I set him down, squatting so that I could better support his head and torso.

"What's the matter with him?" I asked Álvaro.

"Hypnotized," he replied briefly. I waited for him to explain how looking at a ring could throw someone into a trance, but he said nothing more. John stirred and began to mutter.

"There's a light...." he began, clutching my shoulder as though what he was trying to tell me was of great importance. "...a light in the stone...goes round and round...I saw all the world...fast light...took me...all the world. I was around the world...*in* the world...all over...the world was clean...young...mine...sky was blue...a deep, deep...deep blue...falling into the blueness...long way...teeming...life all over the world...my life...no man at all...and there was...the fields were green...all green...and the mountains were unscarred...and the sea was clean and clear...and the winds were fresh...and the sun shone and shone...there was no night...and rainbows were dancing...it rained so clear, like jewels...no roads...no villages...no churches...no taverns...no houses...no spires...no lights...no men...and it moved...as I wanted it to move...all moved...and there was a voice...a tiny voice...a voice below...beneath...and it said...create...create me...I will serve...born to serve...create me...you are God...create...create...."

"He's coming out of it," said Álvaro, as John began to move again, tossing as though in restless sleep. His voice lost its faint, atonal quality.

"I don't believe it," said John deliberately. Almost instantly, the mood was gone. He was completely himself again.

I helped him to his feet, and looked concerned, but he nodded to assure me that he was all right.

I looked back at the giant. He was flickering his fingers back and forth over his face. As they fluttered over his eyes, he closed them. Then, the fingers returned to the statue, and began to shape the clay into a face—his *own* face.

"So that's why the statues have such strange eyes," I murmured. John coughed, still a little dizzy from his abrupt return to reality.

We walked back slowly to the road, where Darling waited with dispassionate patience.

Suddenly, the giant stood up, apparently to watch us leave. He was stark naked, and I felt my eyebrows rise with astonishment.

The skin around the giant's groin was smooth and unbroken. I had paused, and John had to half-drag me up on to the wheel, and back to my position with the reins.

"But look at him," I protested.

"So what?"

I still couldn't quite believe it. I shook the reins reflexively, and Darling hauled us away before I was quite ready to go.

"What sort of creature *was* he?" I demanded to know.

"A man," said Álvaro. "Only a man."

"A god," corrected John, "so long as he wears that ring. A maker of men."

"Only in his own mind," I said.

There was no reply. After a short pause, John said, to himself I think, "And God made man in his own image."

"So it seems," I said, glancing sideways as we passed yet another of the blind statues, which stood calmly by the roadside, its right arm raised in ironic farewell. "But I thought there were no gods any longer. The Brotherhood says not." I inclined my head slightly toward Brother Álvaro.

"Our Brotherhood is not concerned with the existence or otherwise of deities," he replied. "Such things matter not at all. We deny nothing. We concern ourselves only with the affairs of man and Afterman."

"Tell me," I said, daring to trust him for the first time, "what is an Afterman? A blind being, perhaps—without sex—who is carved from clay? Or a maker of statues, with a ring which assures him that he is God?"

"Matthew," he said. "You mock. And you mock. I know that you have stayed silent and listened to your brother and myself while we argue. And I know that you have no sympathy with either of us, nor even with the fact that we bother to argue. You are a settled man, with no ambitions, no need for change. Because of that, you can never find the truth."

"No indeed," I agreed jovially, but regretting somewhat that I had been tempted to speak in the first place. "The truth will never trouble me. Nor shall falseness."

"The Afterman is a real truth, Matthew."

"Then what *is* he?" I demanded. "What springs from our progeny to make us obsolete?"

"'A being of the mind," said Álvaro. "A being born without preconceptions, so that his person may be wholly responsive to reality, and will not prejudge. You and I, you see, are preconditioned by instinct, and because we must learn from our parents. The animals are even more restricted, for they learn very little, and are almost complete before they are even born.

"Evolution, I think, works with the young. Man is born while he still has twenty years to develop—twenty years to adjust to and accept new realities, to use new perceptions. His brain forms *along with his experiences*, and the two link into a coherent whole—the mind. The Afterman will be the next step in that succession, or so I believe. Remember, of course, that it is not given to us to *know*.

"The Afterman will not be conditioned by genes. Man is a step removed from the animals in that he may *control*, to a degree, the environment which shapes him. The Afterman, I think, must be a step beyond that, in that he must be *removed* entirely from the influence of that environment. He will be *free*."

"It's a fine dream," admitted John. He was still slightly affected by his own opportunity to be a god. Perhaps, for a while, he would have an understanding of what it meant to be free. The similarity between what John had said while in his trance, and what Álvaro had described as a being free of his environment, had not escaped me.

"It's a dream of ideas and words, though," I reminded him. "You say yourself that you will not see, that you cannot know."

"You have no dreams yourself," corrected Álvaro. "Yet how does it fit into your worldly wisdom that a deformed man without sex can make statues?"

"He can," I admitted, "but I don't see what you're driving at. What is...*is*. What is not, remains speculation. It's nothing to me."

"He calls me a madman," John said to Álvaro—and I wondered whether I had not been *too* ridiculous, if I were forcing the two to agree—"because I am not happy. Because I have beliefs and ambitions, because I have a need. He can never be convinced of any truth. He is dead in all but that he breathes."

"I'm happy," I added.

John scowled, but Álvaro laughed.

VII.

THE DREAM

Álvaro left us the next morning, after profuse apologies for having presumed upon our charity for so long. I was sorry to see him go—I'd liked the little man despite all the arguing he'd put us through. Even John wasn't pleased to see this particular hindrance removed, and he usually liked things to be as simple as possible.

As he waved goodbye, he called something about seeing us again someday. We were well up into the mountains by this time, above the tree line and into the land of bare rock and chilly, noisy winds. The road went on, and was more distinct here—not because it was used, but because there was little living wildness to encroach upon it and repossess it.

I did not like this kind of country—characterless and deathly, all ridge and wall and scree. But it was all the same to John, merely an honest part of a whole world full of desolation.

We know now that we had almost caught the man we followed. He moved slowly still, and we were so far now from any decent land that his destination became sure. To the east of the gigantic Peak of Sorrows lay three less formidable crags set in an equilateral triangle—the Peak of Wrath, the Peak of Storms and the Peak of the Thunderer. On the slopes of the last-named, was a village named Hawkeyrie, to which he had returned not three days before us. John's hopes were high, and even I felt anticipation at the prospect of ending our quest.

There was only one more village between ourselves and Hawkeyrie—one more resting place for one more night. Then Hawkeyrie and a destination.

It was during the last minutes of twilight that we rumbled down a loose stone slope into the village, whose name we never discovered. From the main street, the nearest of the three peaks—the Peak of Storms—was easily visible, and the Peak of the Thunderer could be seen beyond its left shoulder.

We could see nothing of the valley between the three peaks, into which the road would take us tomorrow. We had heard that eternal mists shrouded the valley floor, and that when the mountain men wished to go to Hawkeyrie, they went the hard way—over the top. Darling, of course, would have to go by road, and so we could not follow the man who walked through time precisely. But neither John nor I was afraid of a mist-filled valley, even though the mountain people mentioned it with superstitious reluctance.

Lights burned brightly up and down the main street and along the three tiny side-alleys. Associating the highest lights with a hostel and a bed for the night, I pulled up before a tall building with many windows. It was unmarked, which was odd, for hostels were almost invariably taverns as well, and taverns usually have names, but I thought nothing of this at the time, and dismounted to shove at the door. John hitched Darling to a post in the street, and joined me while I registered surprise that the door did not yield to my hand.

We were both very tired, and thinking slowly.

John pushed too, then shrugged and rapped loudly on the door. A few seconds passed while we looked at each other wondering what to do next, and we realized that this was neither a tavern nor a travelers' hostel. A haggard face was thrust from the gloom and eyes peered from heavy lids, drinking in our appearance.

"'Ang me," said the man. "Strangers, bigawd. Well?" The voice was hoarse and whistled slightly because of a shortage of teeth.

"I'm sorry," I began. "We wanted a room for the night and mistook your home for an inn."

"'Eh?'" questioned the other. I wasn't sure whether he'd not heard me, or whether he was just stupid.

"A room for the night," said John. "Have you one?"

The eyelids drooped even further, and the door began to close. Then the other apparently underwent a change of heart, for it opened again. "Nime?" he inquired.

"John, the Firefly."

"Eh?"

"Firefly. This is Matthew, my brother."

"Oh."

A long weary pause, while we tried to fathom out what the old man required of us.

"Hah!" he said, at last, apparently making up his mind. "Ya wanna 'scape?"

John apparently interpreted this as an inquiry as to whether he desired to escape from the world, for he answered, "Yes."

"Cautious bleeder," remarked the old one. "Ne'er saw ya 'fore. Dinna know who sent yer. In!"

The door opened wide. I was sure that there had been a breakdown in communication, and that we were talking at cross-purposes with the villager, but John was already inside, and I followed him.

The door slammed behind me, and both bolts slid ominously shut. I wondered vaguely who or what they were intended to keep out. Or in.

A lamp flared into life, and the bestial creature looked up at us, giving me a beaming grin which showed about three rotting brown molars and a vast expanse of frayed gum. I winced, and wished we'd stayed outside.

"C'mn in," he said, as if we were his oldest friends. "We 'ready started. Jussa fing for yer." He halted suddenly. "Y' can pay?"

"For the room?" countered John.

The other beamed again. "Allin," he said.

"All what?"

"Oller? Oller?" said the old man, quite incomprehensibly. "Kri' man. Ya wanna 'scape or no?"

John brightened at the second mention of escape. His mind returned to its one safe track.

54

"You can get me back in time?"

"Back 'n time, forward 'n time, t'other side 'f it. 'Ere or there 'r werreva y'like. Can ya pay?"

"Can you prove what you say?" said John. We were both totally bewildered. This was obviously not the man who walked through time, yet he seemed to be offering us an escape through time. The dwarfish man looked puzzled at the request for proof, and John turned back to me, lifting a hand to indicate the bolted door. The other man suddenly erupted in agitation.

"Pay later," he said. "Don't go."

"Later?" said John, incredulously. *"You mean afterwards?"*

"Let's get out of here," I said. But the dwarf drowned me out. "Yar, 'kay, 'kay. Afterw'ds, later, when y'done."

John was puzzled but deeply intrigued.

"Will I be able to go wherever I like?" he asked.

"Anywhere," stressed the dwarf. "Y'can take yer bloody warhorse too, f'r all I care."

"Lead the way," said John.

"No!" I protested.

"Come on," urged John. "You're twice his size. What on earth can he do to us?"

For all I knew, he might have fifty brothers upstairs. I remembered the lights at the windows. *Something* was going on, and curiosity wasn't going to trap *me*.

"No," I said.

John grabbed me by the arm and pulled me. I resisted.

"Look," he said. "What can happen? Don't you even want to know?"

"No."

"All right then. I'll go by myself."

The dwarf had shambled down the corridor carrying the lamp, had mounted the first three steps of an ascending staircase, and had turned to await our attendance. John strode after him, and I followed, fearful of what might happen.

I wished that John had brought his crossbow, although the clumsy device could hardly have been useful in here.

Damp dripped from the ceiling; cockroaches and wood lice scuffled in the crevices as the light scared them back into hiding. We passed several rooms from whose ill-fitting doors filtered filmy light. I was glad to note that the doors had neither locks nor outside bolts.

Eventually, about three flights up, the dwarf opened a door and ushered us into a tiny, square room without any furniture except for two beds. I exhaled with some relief. Could the weird creature have been offering us a bed for the night after all? By the dim lantern light, I saw that John was vaguely disappointed.

The dwarf set the lantern down in the middle of the floor and scuttled from the room. I reached out and pulled the door to behind him.

"Well," I said. "what do you make of that?"

"Don't you ever tire of asking that?" he retorted testily. "You know just as much as I do!"

"But *you* were talking to him," I protested. "You must have some idea what he was going on about. It was your idea, damn it!"

He shrugged. "Hadn't the faintest idea," he admitted. "But nothing wrong with finding out."

"Oh, no!" I said. "Nothing at all. We get welcomed like this every place we go. How else would we ever find beds for the night?"

"Ha, ha," he said, humorlessly.

"And what was all that about escape?"

"I don't know. Are you sure it was 'escape' he said?"

"Am I sure? You were the one who wanted...."

"Oh, shut up!" he said, and flopped down onto one of the beds. He prodded it suspiciously. "Well," he judged, "it might not be clean, but it's not crawling either. Mountain men wash, it seems. I'm tired."

I gave up, and sat down on the other bed, looking at him. He affected to be unaware of my presence, and gave every appearance of preparing for sleep. I cursed silently, and lay back, staring at the pitted ceiling, still trying to work out what had happened.

"Shall I put the lamp out?" asked John.

"No!" I growled. That reminded me of the lights burning in all the other rooms. I sat up again.

The dwarf shambled back into the room, holding something in his hand. I couldn't see what it was, because he crossed in front of the lamp and it fell into shadow.

"'Old still," said the dwarf, and stabbed me.

It took an unconscionably long time to register. Something sharp had been shoved into my arm. But the attitude of the man was so unsuited to that of a murderer. He acted as though what he had done was perfectly in order, turning away and going across to the other bed. It must have been five or six seconds before I reacted.

"Hey!" I bawled, and then, to John: "Be careful!"

"'S'awright," the dwarf was saying, batting John's hand down with a hairy fist. "'Old it fer kri' sake."

"Wahya doin'?" I snarled, hearing my voice slur horribly as I tried to rise. "Leave'm alone!"

There was a sudden biting pain, and a fierce heat. Dimly, I saw John kick the dwarf in the face and take away the stiletto from his hand. Then....

A deep mist, whose particles were scintillating motes of silver and gilt, descended, cutting off all sound. Through the dust floated tiny patterns of intangible thread, which adhered to my skull and passed through into the pulsing convolutions of my brain. I could hear my own heart beating like a panicked drum, drowning out my frantic thoughts. Then it was dying, and peace fondled my thrilling eardrums, erasing my anger and the sharp hollow pain which had seized my arm.

Down, down, down, I felt my brain falling, as though it were disappearing down my throat and through my bowels. Colors exploded into my eyes, shimmering into whirling rainbows, swaying and weaving.

I was standing on a mound of green turf, and all around me, in fantastic complexity, was a vast city. It shimmered and glowed in the caressing sunlight, like the colors had. A million curtained windows reflected light like the facets of a dark diamond.

It was all so beautiful, so wonderful.

Awe seized my brain and denied me proper thought. I was totally possessed by an emotional surge whose like I had never experienced before. My broken heart ached from the strain, and I began to cry.

The walls—billions of *clean* metal walls—vibrated to a hidden melody with *movement,* such movement as I had never dreamed could exist. All the people in the world gathered in a single plaza, all dancing and living at top speed, could not have made half the movement that was in the city.

High above the city flew glinting sparks, like bursting fireworks, or a huge flock of hummingbirds. My head spun with the sheer immensity of the buildings and the life and the people. A man came to help me up.

"Excuse me," I said, "but can you tell me what year it is?" I knew the figure would be meaningless, but I wished to savour it in my ears. The man ignored the question. I couldn't see his face.

"Remember," whispered a close, cool voice, "that things that you do not understand are not necessarily lies."

I whirled round. "Queen of The Red Wolf!" She roared with hysterical mirth, and shrank into the distance as if borne away by wings.

"This city had everything. Someday it will belong to the cats and the rats and the bats. Then we will climb, my species and I, to infinity."

I turned to the incredibly old man, who was growing into a giant. My own voice shrieked at me: "You're God? Who told you that?"

"My fire is small, but it has not your consuming passion," said the father Sun from the sky, and then disappeared, leaving the world to night.

"Never fear, Firefly," said a new voice. "Our warrior can take care of this."

"But I'm not the Firefly," I protested. "I'm Matthew."

"I love you," said my shadow.

"Y'wanna 'scape? Y'wanna 'scape?"

"Sometimes, one has to stand silent."

Álvaro!

"To conquer, you see, you have to make something a part of you. We cannot tell how high the tree might grow, or if it will ever stop. Our time is over, John."

"I'm not John. I'm Matthew."

"You mock. And you mock. You can never find the truth."

"Álvaro, please help me!"

Silence.

"Who are you, candle?"

Faintly. No one near.

"Where are you going?"

"Who are you?"

"All the world's happy."

"I am the Firefly, because the sun's light gives life to everything on Earth, and I have life beyond that, and thus cast a light of my own. I go my own way. I am the Firefly."

"John! John, are you there? Help me?"

"Matthew!" Very, very far away. I couldn't see. "Wake up!"

"Y'can't. Y'can't." Snivelling.

"ARE YOU HAPPY?" A shout in my ear. My voice.

"Happy?"

"Happy?"

I cried out in anguish. At once, the air was still and empty. All the disembodied voices had been swept away. There was a profound cemetery silence. I looked up. There was nothing there (where?) so I stood up. There was no one in sight. I looked at the wide open door nearby.

In bold letters, it was marked EXIT.

I stared, fascinated, at the dark opening. I moved closer to it, and peered into the gloom beyond, careful not to cross the threshold.

Hesitantly, I extended a foot.

A harsh voice said, "You cannot come this way. sir. One way only."

"I want to get out."

"Sorry sir. Can you not see that the door is clearly marked EXIT?"

"But that's what I want to do."

There was a silence.

"Sir?" said the door politely.

"Yes?" I returned, hopefully.

"Kindly shut the door. Notice that EXIT is on the *inside*. You cannot leave this way."

"But I want to go back."

"There's no light there."

"I cast my own."

"I'm sorry sir. It is impossible."

"I want to escape."

"I would not try if I were you, sir."

"So you wouldn't. Do I care?"

"No sir, and that is part of the problem. Running away serves no real purpose, sir."

"I'm Matthew, not John."

"It does not matter, sir, what your name might or might not be." There was silence. I pushed the door. It was locked. That was wrong.

I tried to remember it being open, but I could not. Nor could I remember it closing.

I sat down, and wept silently. The word EXIT glowed mutely. As tears blurred my vision, my eyes opened and lantern-light blasted the darkness apart. A dark hand snatched it away.

"Matthew," said John eagerly. "Are you all right?"

"Awri', awri'," mumbled the hoarse voice of the dwarf in the background. "'Ow was it?" he continued. "Sat'sfied, I bet, huh? Like it?"

"You tricked me! It wasn't real. Not any of it. All a fraud. I'll kill you." I realized that it was me speaking.

John sat down beside me, and gripped my shoulders.

"Matthew, it's all right. It was a drug. No harm done. I've seen the others—half a hundred of them. All dreaming pleasant dreams. Nothing to worry about."

There was a dull sting in my arm where the needle had gone in.

"Wass' marrer?" babbled the dwarf. "Don't 'urt. On'y a drug. 'Armless. Everyone like it. Wass' marrer? Makes people 'appy. Wass' marrer?" The words rushed out in a bubbling torrent.

"Shut up or I'll slit your throat!" hissed John.

"Escape," I murmured. "Some escape!"

"Go to sleep now. I'll watch this one. If he's hurt," I heard him say to the dwarf, "I'm going to kill you."

"Now," bleated the frightened creature. "On'y save 'em. No 'urt. From 'emselves, y'see? From th'r weakness an'uselessness. Gi'm a lit'l t'make'm 'appy. Why can't y'be 'appy? Why dn'y'want any?"

"Because it's all false. It's all unreal."

"What isn't?" I heard the dwarf say.

John lowered me back on to the bed, and I slept.

Dreamlessly, I think.

VIII.

CROSSROADS OF THE WORLD

When I awoke, it was daylight again, although the lamp still burned in the middle of the room. It seemed even more drab by daylight than it had the previous night. The walls were stained and their angles caked with cobwebs and filth. The ancient skirting boards were cracked and warping away from the damn walls. The beds were hollowed in the middle, and the blankets were old and dirty.

John lay beside me on the bed, his head beside my feet, his own feet dangling just above the floorboards. He was asleep. I sat up slowly, and he jerked suddenly into life, looking round him.

"I'm sorry," he said. "I didn't mean to sleep."

"No harm done," I said. I felt my arm. There was still a faint sensation of pain, and I rolled up my sleeve to examine the wound. There was a red discoloration and some swelling, but it did not look as bad as I'd feared.

"I only hope that needle was clean," I muttered.

"Do you want to stay here for a while and make sure you're all right?" asked John.

"Here?" I said, looking around with theatrical disgust.

"In the village," he corrected.

I looked at him carefully. He meant it. By tonight, or tomorrow at the latest, we should be in Hawkeyrie. Yet John was willing to wait another day.

"No," I said. "I'm all right."

"Sure?"

"Sure. Now let's get out of here."

I rose to my feet carefully, but the drug had left no after-effects that I could detect. My head was clear, and my movements normal.

John rose too, and pushed open the door for me to pass out of the room and onto the staircase. The lamps still burned here as well. The corridor had no windows, and therefore they were necessary.

We made our way down, trying to be quiet. The stairs creaked and groaned beneath our weight, and when we got to the bottom, the dwarf was waiting for us. He, too, looked worse by daylight—he was not so frightening but he was nauseating. His face slanted and he carried his head at a peculiar angle. His lips were large and greasy, his eyes set close and always rolling within orbits.

"Pay, huh?" he whispered. He didn't sound too hopeful. I shoved past him and drew back the bolts in the door.

I glanced back in time to see John spit on the floor. "There's payment!" he said. His eyes were blazing, and he looked as though he were on the brink of committing murder.

"Come on," I said quietly.

He gave the dwarf one last glance of loathing, and then we walked out of the door together.

Darling looked at us reproachfully, as if to remind us that we'd somehow contrived to leave her hitched to the wagon all night.

"I'll take care of her," said John. "You take a look around, if you want to."

The sun had risen only a short time before, and the village was not yet awake. In fact, it seemed almost dead. All the houses were dilapidated. Windows were smashed, bricked or boarded. Paint peeled off doors. Slats were missing from virtually every roof. How on earth do they make a living? I wondered. No crops, that's for sure. Sheep and goats, no doubt, on the slopes. Timber a little lower down, if they can be bothered to haul it up from the tree line. But apart from that, what? And why?

I left the village and wandered up a slope to a point from which I could see over the shoulder of the Peak of Storms, into the triangular bowl through which the road ran. I could see nothing except the mist I had been told to expect.

Disappointed, I sat down on the ridge and hurled stones down the slope, aiming at the rooftops far below me. The first four missed and ricocheted off of the mountainside. The fifth one. which did hit a roof, smashed three slates and went clean through. Guiltily, I stopped.

I could see John leading Darling back from the water trough. I watched him prepare her feed and then sit back with uncharacteristic patience to wait for her to eat.

I sighed, and began to go back down again.

It was late morning when we left, but as we rattled down the main street, still no one paid us any heed. People were visible now, and the silence had given way to a discontinuous conglomeration of familiar sounds. but even so, I could not say that the village had come to life. In truth, I suppose, this was very little different from any other village, but the dolefulness and indolence held a quality of ugliness which I had seen nowhere else in the world. It was a foul place.

I was quite glad once we had topped the saddle-shaped ridge between the Peak of Storms and the Peak of the Thunderer, and the village was hidden from our view.

Almost immediately, the mists enveloped us. We could see for only a few yards to either side. The road was invisible, and I was forced to go forward and lead the black mare, because I dared not trust her to make her own way in perfect safety.

After twenty minutes or so of absolute sameness, we came upon a hump-backed bridge. I stopped the horse, and went forward to test it, in case it should be so old that it would no longer support a wagon's weight.

I peered over the stone wall that bordered the bridge, but could see no sign of what lay beneath. I picked up a pebble and lobbed it over the side, expecting to hear a splash. Instead, there was a distinct click.

"That's odd," I said, loud enough for John to hear.

"What is?"

"There's no water down there. This bridge doesn't go over anything."

"The stream may have dried up."

"No, it was rock. The pebble struck something hard. Couldn't you hear?" John lobbed a pebble of his own, which he had picked up from beside the wagon. When that one, too, clicked instead of splashing, he came to join me.

"Does it matter?" he asked.

"It's only a few feet. I want to take a look."

"Don't jump," he said.

I had, of course, no intention of jumping. I made my way round by the side of the bridge, scrambling unsteadily down the steep slope. When I got to the bottom, I looked up. I could just make out the dark shape of John's head and shoulders as he leaned over the lip of the bridge.

"Well?" he asked.

"It's another road," I explained.

"Oh," he said, as though we were fools not to have thought of it. "That's all right then."

"Maybe," I said. "But why's there another road *here*? There's only Hawkeyrie and the north, and we're travelling along that road. There's nowhere for this one to go. Or come from, for that matter."

"So it's old," he said, with a hint of annoyance. "So what? Let's get on."

I clambered back up the bank, and regained the bridge.

We led Darling across without causing the bridge the slightest trouble, and continued on our way, one of us on either side of Darling's head.

After a further half mile, I asked, "Can you see your edge of the road?"

"No," he replied, without stopping.

"Neither can I," I supplied.

"So?"

"Five minutes ago I could see both sides."

"So, the road's getting wider," he replied with devastating logic. I shook my head, without really knowing why.

Three miles further on, I insisted we stop.

"Why?" John wanted to know.

"Because I haven't seen the roadside for an age and a half. I've got my doubts as to whether we're still *on* a road."

"Well, don't go too far. We can do without your getting lost. And in any case, we certainly haven't come *off* the road."

He was right. Some fifteen yards to my right was a ragged line demarcating thick green grass from grey stone road.

"There's a light up ahead," called John as I stood staring at the edge and wondering what I was worrying about.

I peered into the mist, but could see nothing. I heard the wagon wheels grind as they began to roll forward again.

"Hey!" I yelled. "Wait for me."

By the time I'd caught up, I could see the light as well. Then, appearing like magic from the grey curtains of the fog, it resolved itself into a lamp held by a tall, thin man. He was dressed with what might have passed for sartorial elegance in these parts. He stopped, and surveyed us, idly swinging his lamp from one finger.

"Who are you?" he asked. His voice was warm and pleasant. He sounded glad to see us.

"We're travellers bound for Hawkeyrie."

"Oh!" He sounded disappointed. "Hawkeyrie."

"We didn't know anyone lived down here," I said, to make conversation. "I'm Matthew, and this is my brother John."

"I'm Conrad. The guide."

"Guide? Then you don't live down here?"

"Yes, I do."

"Well who do you guide, then?" I inquired.

"Anyone who wants guidance."

I looked about me. at the mist. "It can't be very pleasant living down here," I said. "Don't you ever want to see the sun?"

"Sometimes. I go to Hawkeyrie. But come, we mustn't stand *here* talking. My house is just a little further on. No doubt you could do with a hot drink."

I could indeed, and John didn't leap to protest, as he might have done on another day.

"We want to find a man who can walk through time," said John.

"Oh, *him*. Yes, I saw him a while ago. Went up old Thunder, he did. Don't know for sure that he was headed for Hawkeyrie, though. Said something about a lodge near the summit."

"Can't be much to hunt way up here," I commented.

"Oh, the trees grow higher on old Thunder than anywhere else hereabouts. Woods all over the slopes. Beautiful country."

I remembered that he hadn't yet explained why he lived down here, although he hadn't actually seemed to avoid the question either.

"Exactly what do you *do* down here?" I asked.

"I'm a Guide," he replied, with an infuriating calm. He wasn't trying to be difficult, I could see that. He meant what he said.

"Here we are," he said, as a tall shadow loomed out of the mist. I had barely glanced at it before we were ushered in through the door.

His house was as neat as his clothing, everything was in perfect order. It was quite the most pleasant dwelling I had seen in our years of wandering.

We sat down in ageless armchairs which were soft and springy, and sipped good tea from cups which must have been old a hundred years before.

"It's marvellous," I said. "But why down here?"

He laughed. "Where else?"

"Up in the mountains. If the Thunderer is as beautiful as you say, why not there?"

"Because this is the crossroads of the world. I'm the guide. I look after it."

I had a sudden inspiration. "How many roads lead away from here?"

"Six."

"And how many more cross the valley?"

"Thirty."

"Thirty! But why?"

He didn't seem to see any answer to that. His blankness of expression said plainly, "Why not?"

"But there's nowhere for them to go," I said. "They must all stop at the edge of the valley—on the ridges between the peaks."

He looked a little discomfited, as if I had mentioned something not quite fit for polite conversation.

"Not *now*," he agreed. "But this is still the crossroads of the world."

"And you direct the traffic?"

"That's right. I can tell you the direction of any city in the world. And how far it is."

"Langley," I said. It wasn't a city, but a small town. It was the place where I was born.

"That way," he said, pointing. "One hundred sixty-three miles."

I could tell the distance was in the right region, and might have been precise. The direction was good as well. I believed him.

"Paris," I said.

"That way," he announced confidently. "Four hundred eleven miles."

"But what's the point," asked John, "if the roads don't go there anymore?"

Conrad looked pained, as though his toes had been stepped on. "It's my job," he said.

Not so much a job, I decided, as a purpose in life. A borrowed purpose, perhaps. A futile one, no doubt. But sufficient purpose to *support* a man. Like a God who made statues. Like a man who called himself the Sun. Like the brother of the Afterman. Like a man with a young brother. But not like the Firefly, who had only a dream.

"Which way is Hawkeyrie?" asked John.

"That way," said the tall man, eager to please. "Seven miles, no more. And the road *does* go there," he added, with a hint of triumph. It no doubt made his day to be able to put a couple of travelers on the right road.

IX.

PEAK OF THE THUNDERER

We reached Hawkeyrie before nightfall, but discovered—much to John's chagrin—that Conrad had been right, and that the man who walked through time had gone further on, up the Peak of the Thunderer, to a small stone hut near the summit.

So we were forced to spend another restless night. Having had little sleep the previous night, John was already irritable, and when the nearness of our confrontation with the time-walker threatened to rob him of a second night's sleep, his fidgeting became well nigh unbearable. We slept fitfully, in two tiny cots in a small boarding house. Hawkeyrie was quiet, but possessed none of the deathly quality of our previous overnight resting-place.

Nevertheless, I was glad when the village was behind us and we were once more on our way on what, surely, must be the last leg of our journey.

The road was steep but not unduly difficult. The woods to either side were unnaturally thick with vegetation, and I reasoned this to be because this slope of the Peak of the Thunderer was the only one on any of the three mountains which had an unshadowed southern aspect.

The day was warm, and the air pleasantly laden with the scents of a dying summer.

I was beginning to forget the recent past and commit myself wholly to the enjoyment of life once again, when an arrow came from nowhere to drill a hole through Darling's skull.

The old mare simply folded up, without a sound. The reins slipped from my hands as I stood, aghast, looking at the suddenly still corpse which the shafts of the wagon would not allow to fall.

Without raising his head, John had whipped the crossbow up from between his knees and loaded it with a simultaneous fluid action. But the damned thing took so long to wind that he never had a chance to use it.

"Throw the crossbow away," commanded a voice which came from the tangled undergrowth bordering the road. I twisted my head, trying to peer down through the greenery to catch a glimpse of the speaker, but I could see nothing. John made no move to obey the order, but stopped turning the crosskey.

Something moved, and the demand was repeated. John retained his loose hold on the weapon.

"Why did you shoot my horse?" I called. "There was no reason to do that." Silence.

"We've nothing of value." I added.

The archer came into view, stepping out from the depths of a thick bush. It was a woman, dressed in shabby clothes and wearing an overgarment which seemed to have been stitched from half a dozen animal pelts of different sorts.

"The horse is food," she said briefly. "And if you don't throw the crossbow away, we'll be eating *you* too."

"Food!" said John incredulously. "But there's plenty of game in these woods. There's no shortage of food in Hawkeyrie!"

He paused to drop the crossbow over the side of the wagon as the woman raised her bow to aim.

"There's no necessity to go round shooting travelers and their mounts," he added.

"I'm no huntress," said the woman bitterly. "I've a child to care for. Easy meat is the only kind I've time to get. If that's travelers' horses, then hard luck on the travelers. It's a traveler's child, in any case."

"No husband?" queried John.

She gave him a scathing look. "Never had one. Stranger was here a year or two back. Always said he'd come back.

70

Did, too—three days or so back. But he wasn't interested in children. Different things on *his* mind."

"Did this man ever speak of walking through time?"

"Never stopped," said the woman disgustedly. "Mad, he was. Still is."

"Where is he?"

"Why? You friends of his?" The arrow was now aimed at my stomach. I winced.

"No," I broke in.

"But we're looking for him," added John.

"He's at the hut up on top," she spoke, as if she hoped he'd never come down again. "But he won't be there long. Day or two and he'll be off again. No time for *us*."

"Point the arrow somewhere else," I requested. "We're not going to do you any harm."

"No, you're not. You can walk up the mountain." She paused, looking defiantly at me. Then she lowered the weapon. "I'm sorry about the horse," she said. "But I do need meat. Badly."

"Won't they help you in Hawkeyrie?"

"They don't like outsiders."

"But surely...," I began.

"I'm not going begging," she retorted sharply.

"No," said John harshly, "you're going thieving and murdering instead."

"I've killed nobody."

"Not yet. And not far off either."

She was still angry, but she made no move to threaten us with the weapon again. I got the impression that she was on the verge of tears.

"Get on with you," she said. her voice raised to a near-shout. "Up the mountain. Go on. Find your precious friend and tell him I hope he rots."

I got down slowly from the wagon. John dismounted on the other side and moved towards his crossbow.

"Leave it alone," she ordered.

"Come on," I said. "We don't need that."

"What about the wagon?" he asked.

"If you want to haul it, go ahead," I said. "Otherwise. we'll let this charming young lady steal what she wants from it, and we'll pick up everything we need—and can carry—on the way back down."

"If we ever come back down," he said, in a low voice.

We cast resentful and accusing looks at the woman, and began the long walk. I looked down at Darling as I passed her head.

"Old lady," I said under my breath, "you brought us here. You made it. I'm sorry."

It was a long, hard road up to the top. From Hawkeyrie to the peak wasn't a great distance, as the crow flies. But it was all uphill—and a very steep hill at that. We were both fit and strong, but even so, we tired rapidly.

The dirt road became a track, and finally petered out into a thin footpath. It began to curl round the mountain instead of going on up, and we never actually came within a mile of the topmost crag.

We stopped to rest, finally, when the sun had worn us down to the point where even John couldn't continue. We sat down, side by side, unsmiling and silent, contemplating the view. We could see for miles and miles. The stark Peaks of Wrath, Storms and Sorrows were all to the north and east of us, and the southward outlook consisted of an ocean of undulating green moors, rivers and forests. We could see no roads, but occasional plumes of dull smoke gave evidence of villages nestled out of sight in the valleys.

A walking stick jabbed its point into the soft earth between us. "It's a beautiful world," said the man who walked through time, "but the sun makes your eyes ache if you look too long."

We both looked up at him, and neither of us could think of anything to say. My first impression was one of surprise, that this man could look so ordinary. He was medium in just about all things—height, build, complexion, hair color...even his eyes were a muddy, characterless brown. They fixed upon John.

"You are the Firefly," he said. "The caster of light."

"You know me, then?" replied John.

"People remembered you."

"You too."

"But not for the same reason." The man who walked through time smiled paternally.

"Why didn't you wait for us, if you knew we were following?" John asked.

I rose to my feet and walked across to the lip of the slope, on the far side of the path. It was all theirs, now. I felt like an intruder.

"Why should I inconvenience myself? I had a quest, just like you. I was hoping you'd give up the search, too. I nearly left messages for you at Hawkeyrie, and one or two other places. But I guessed that you'd come on anyway. So I went my way, and let you catch up in your own good time.

"I can't do it, you know," he added.

"Can't do what?"

I could hear the fear in John's voice. To have come so far, and only to find the answer I'd suspected all along.

"Take you back in time, or show you how to do it. Time travel backwards is impossible. It's not really me that travels, you see. It's Time itself. And Time goes its own way. Nobody can bring it back for a second attempt."

"You mean that all your fine stories were nothing but a pack of lies?" His heart must have been broken, poor child. But he carried on. No anger. No remorse...just questions and more questions. Always searching.

"No, not lies. I've been there, to these marvelous places you want to go. I belong there, I suppose. But I left them, and I don't regret doing so. I came away, and now there's no road back. It's not for me to tell you what's right for you and what's not, but it really might be all for the best. You wouldn't like it. Nobody could. Too much pressure. You can't have struggle and peace as well."

"I don't want *peace.* I want life."

"You don't know what you want."

"I know what I *don't* want," said John, all his bitterness brimming over and beginning to pour out. "I don't want *this* world. I don't want *now.*

"This world is dead. I don't know why. I think it's something to do with time. Time doesn't seen to *happen* any more. Everything just drifts. No tomorrow—not even a today—just a million yesterdays and everybody drenched with contentment. There's no future any more—nothing that people will work for.

"You want to go over the next hill? Why? It's pretty much the same as here. You wonder what the stars are? They're worlds. So what? You want to know why that man does that? Why? It won't benefit you. If you want to do it too, go ahead, nobody cares. Why? Why? Why? There doesn't seem to be any *force* in the world. People don't want to build, they don't even want to destroy. There's a woman down the mountain with a child. She even thinks she ought to take care of it, which is something. But you know what she did? She sat by the road and ambushed our horse. She could walk to Hawkeyrie and find food—get milk for the child. But she doesn't *care* enough to do it. She is where she is and that's where she stays. What sort of a life *is* that?

"This is the world I was born into. Well, it's not *my* world. Matthew's maybe. Big brother Matthew would live in a sewer and not notice the smell. But not me. When I heard about you, I found a chance to get out of it, to go back to the time when there was a living human race, when to be a man meant something more than to be a turnip.

"And what do I find? You can't take me. You can only go forward into a future that can never exist. The whole human race is a breathing cadaver, and I have to watch it rot. Dying with it. And I'm the only poor fool who feels the pain.

"Can I find a life here? No. Not among a people who live solely for illusion. What sort of happiness is it that comes from madness and delusion? From rings and drugs and nothing real? Not me. I'm *real*, and I want real things.

"Oh yes, I could preach what I believe. I could try and teach people. But that's illusion too, or would be—a wandering fanatic threatening damnation on all who don't believe. But actually thinking that someone might listen? And I don't *want* to change anyone else. Why should *they* change when the disease is in *me*? *They're* happy! It's me who isn't. Me! They've achieved what they wanted, and I can't even begin to look. Their happiness is killing them. And I'll die for lack of mine."

"In a way," said the man who walked through time, "you're right. You can't have what everyone else has won. It isn't fair. But what justice is there for you to appeal to? This is the way things are. There's no way round it.

"There's no way back!"

EXIT. On the *other* side of the door. One way only. Poor Firefly, I thought. Poor little Firefly. It does not matter, sir, what your name might or might not be. Impossible.

"There's no way," agreed John. Emotionlessly.

"Cry, you fool!" I wanted to shout. "Weep!" But that wasn't John's way. He'd die without a tear in his eye.

"There's one thing," said the man who walked through time.

"What?"

I didn't dare hope.

"Mankind is dying out because the race has exhausted its potential. There's nothing left. The sands of time have run out. But while mankind dies, something *new* is forming. A new kind of being. Not a new kind of man—not a *Homo superior*, as we've so vainly imagined. Something alien. Something beyond man by as far as man is beyond a lungfish."

"The Afterman."

"The Afterman. You can't be one of them. But you can help them. You can prepare the way for them. You can prolong the dying of man, so that out of that dying can come a new life. No time for us any more...just existence. But for the Afterman—all the time in the world might be only just enough. We have to keep the race of Man in existence. We have to allow the Afterman the time of his birth and maturation. We can *help*, Firefly. We can *do* something.

"When I came here from the trouble-torn past, I expected to find the race of Man ascended to what I'd believed to be his true greatness. But I'd been blinded by pride. There's no such greatness. I walked further and further into time, and found less and less.

"But I'll walk no further now, Firefly. The days and nights can pass me by at their own pace from now until the day I die, because I've found *my* resting place."

"With the Brotherhood of the Afterman," said John scornfully. "With their aims. With their ambitions. They're all that this world holds. All that could possibly mean anything to you or me."

John was silent for a moment. "They're not enough," he said, finally.

"They're the only thing there is."

"I am the Firefly," he said. "I cast my own light."

"In that case," said the man who walked through time, regretfully, "there's nothing more to be said."

"No," agreed John.

He got to his feet, and moved off down the hill, slowly, leaving his slaughtered dreams behind him. I didn't follow. He didn't want the kind of clumsy consolation that wise brother Matthew could offer.

I looked the other man straight in the eyes.

"He'll be back," said the man who walked through time. "There are only happy people down there. And he can never be one of them."

X.

TRAVELLER IN TIME

I returned with the man who walked through time to his little hut on the mountain, and waited with him there till long past nightfall. He ignored me, for the most part. He cooked himself a meal on the ancient stove without offering to let me share it. I would have gone away, as he so obviously wanted me to, but I did not want to find John too soon, and I valued John's feelings far more than those of the man who had so calmly tortured them with wise words and no hope.

Eventually, though, he relented, and we drank some vegetable wine together. He had finished his meal by now, and had little else to do save sit by the fire. I didn't bother to ask what he was doing up here. I could only conclude that it was a way station in his travels. Perhaps the spot had meant something to him in a previous time.

My company was less of a nuisance now that he had nothing to occupy his hands and mind with. I was someone to talk to.

"He'll never come back to you, you know," I said.

He shrugged. "It doesn't matter. I don't want him. My affair is a private one anyhow. He couldn't understand. He can run away again, and welcome. The Afterman doesn't need him. But there's nowhere to run to. It's all finished—the age of man on Earth—and he'll find that there's no escape from obsolescence. The Afterman can. Men can't. We're bound by our miserable selves. We're only animals. We haven't what it takes to be free."

"I don't understand."

"Nor do I—not really. Could a reptile understand a man? But we were reptilian once—your ancestors and mine. So were the first mammals, the first primates. Men will go on, and on, and on, but they'll be the apes and the monkeys of the future. The sterile offshoots, the left-behind. Just animals, with no purpose and no destiny. The *special* men—*my* men—will go on changing, will give birth to new creatures, to new worlds. I'll die, but the seed I plant will grow. Their sons and daughters in ten thousand—ten million—years will not look like men. They won't think like men. They certainly won't *be* men."

"You're not anything to do with what John wants, are you? It's all been a fool's errand."

"Perhaps. If he can't forget his own childish dreams and ambitions, and live in the real world, then yes, it has been a fool's errand."

"You think him childish?"

"Don't you?"

"Sometimes," I conceded. "But there are other times when he seems to be more of a man than all the rest of us. There's a *direction* to his life. He calls himself Firefly, and it's a good name. It's *his* name. He despises me, I think, because I'm *content*. I'm a simple man. There's nothing that I can *want* any more. Whatever the day brings, I accept. I've outgrown *my* childishness. But am I older and wiser, or simply less alive? I'm not really happy—not even some of the time—but even when I'm *unhappy*, I can endure and wait for the neutral state again. He couldn't stand that. To him, unhappiness is a real pain, and happiness a real dream. The neutral state is really *nothing* to him. It can't exist. He only admits to the presence of life. Maybe he is a child, but he's a wonderful child."

"But what he wants isn't real. It's an image of an untrue past, distorted by time and by his mind. It wasn't a paradise, this Golden Age that he speaks of. It was a harsh, ugly world full of strain and friction. This drive he prizes so highly used to burn men up, cripple them and kill them. And even then, most men couldn't *care*. There were always millions like *you*, Matthew, then as now."

"He can't know that," I said.

"I can. I do. I was born there." He lit a pipe and sucked vigorously to make the tobacco burn. "It made fine stories, about itself, about yet other, purely imaginary times and places. But making stories out of realities *spoils* them. Can't he see that? Stories are neat and coherent. They have beginnings and ends and morals. They're distilled to their bare elements. But that's not like life. Life is so much fuller—so full that we can barely touch a tiny fraction of it. That's our problem—we can't *see*. We're blind worms, Matthew, squirming in the dust. Wherever John goes, he still won't find what he's looking for. Even if he *could* go back."

"Finding nothing wouldn't stop him."

There was a brief silence.

"Can't you give him your secret?" I asked. "All right, he can't go back. But there's no hope for him *here*. Not anywhere in this world. Let him at least have new places to look. If nothing else, he can find your Afterman...know *your* truth for the truth it is. Don't we at least owe him whatever we can offer him?"

"I owe him nothing."

"No help at all? You owe him nothing? You'd deny him even what you could give him?"

He stood up, and walked round behind his chair, gripping the back and leaning forward, as though mentally agitated.

"I can't give him anything," he said. "Nothing at all. I lied when I styled myself 'the man who can walk through time.' I did, once, but not any more. I couldn't go on into the future even if I wanted to. And I tell myself that I don't.

"I'm marooned here. I reached the limit of my resources. "I was like *him* once. I was *searching*, trying to find an answer. I searched and I searched. I combed the Golden Age, which he thinks might hold an answer, but I found *nothing*. Sham, façade, false reason, and false hope—that's what his Golden Age was built on. Agony and misery were all it had to offer. So, I looked further. I trekked through time itself.

"I thought that a better way had to come. Despite the inadequacies of what we *were*, what we *had* was so big, so wonderful, that I felt inside me that the whole universe had to be ours—that the secrets of life had to be found someday.

"But I was wrong. Year after year, century after century after century. All the same. What we *were* did not change, and what we had we lost, because it couldn't give us what we wanted. If you'd seen what I saw...if only you could know, then you'd realize that it's all pointless. There *is* no answer because Man just isn't whole enough to *be* an answer.

"When you see your brother again, tell him that. Tell him that I'm sorry too. I'm sorry for what he feels, for what he thinks, for what he thinks he wants. I'm sorry that there's nothing I can give him—not an answer, not a way to travel in time."

"But you could let him go on searching," I insisted. "You could tell him how to go *forwards*."

"I could tell him. But he couldn't do it. You see, it's not as simple as it sounds. I didn't move *bodily* through time. *Time* moved *quantitatively* through me. Subjectively, it comes to the same thing. Objectively, it's very different. Time isn't a dimension along which one can *move*. It's a property of the mind. The clock that registers minutes and hours is only an interpreter, giving an illusion of externality to an experience that takes place only *inside* us. Time *doesn't* always flow at the same rate. We're all calibrated, one against the other, but what actually *happens*, inside us, is very different in each individual. They used to say that a man should see only three score years and ten during his span upon the Earth, but that isn't true. Men have *seen* centuries, millennia. They themselves have been limited each to a single unit of time: a quantum, if you like. The time of the universe isn't a passage measured by the ticking of a clock. It's a whole single entity, composite within the human mind. Man's perception is the limitation, and the only limitation.

"I took a drug that extended my perception and my perspective. But only in one way—"forwards," as we call it. It didn't give me immortality. It didn't give me control. My being is as weak and as short as your own. It has simply been spread thinner over a greater part of time.

"But it's over now. My perception has folded inwards once again. Maybe the effect of the drug was temporary. I don't know. I can't say whether I lost my perception because I *couldn't* see any more, or because I didn't *want* to. It's the same thing, so far as I'm concerned.

"I was receptive to the drug. Your brother might not be. It might affect his mind in a different way. It might kill him. But if he wants to try it, he's got to find it. I don't know where it came from, or how to make it. I don't know where you'd find anyone in this world who knows anything about it."

He lapsed into silence again. So the future might be reached by means of a drug! Perhaps the escape offered to us in the nameless village beyond Hawkeyrie was the escape which John sought after all. But what had the door told me? One way only. You cannot leave this way. Running away serves no purpose.

But nevertheless, drugs there were, and other devices for extending perception. The god who built sexless statues had worn a ring. Someone had supplied that ring. Someone had supplied the drug to the dwarf.

And there was only one possible source...

XI.

TIME OF DYING

As I had predicted, John did not return. I left at about midnight. There was a bright moon, and the mountain air was clear and cold. I supposed that he must have returned to the wagon, in spite of the woman who now had his precious crossbow.

I was right. I found him, in fact, in the woman's house— a small cabin hidden in the trees near to the road where the abandoned wagon stood. The woman had apparently relented slightly in her hatred of travellers, sufficiently to have offered shelter to the boy. John's mind had been on weightier things than rancor about a dead horse or a stolen crossbow. So soon was poor Darling forgotten.

The woman and child slept, peacefully and apparently without fear, the crossbow by her side.

John and I sat by the fire, peering into the flames. He was lost in the deepness of his thoughts, and I waited patiently for him to return.

It was some time before I noticed that there was a fifth person in the hut. He had been asleep when I arrived but he was alert now. Probably it was his presence that had prompted the woman to allow John to share the comforts of her hearth. Almost certainly it was by virtue of his presence that she herself slept without fear of reprisal from her erstwhile victim.

It was Álvaro.

"You've come still further out of your way," I said. My voice was a little cold. Why was he here?

"Perhaps not," he replied. "A little thought changed my route. I followed you."

"Why?"

"I anticipated your brother's disappointment."

"So."

I squatted down by the fire, warming my hands, and looked at him. He moved forward slowly, and sat down beside me, looking across at John. John moved slightly to allow us more room, but did not break from his intense contemplation.

"I think you knew a long time ago about my brother's disappointment," I said slowly.

The firelight reflected from his spectacles made it difficult to see his eyes, and I could not read his expression.

"Yes," he said. "Perhaps I did. Perhaps I should have."

"You said nothing. You argued with him, but you didn't tell him it was impossible."

"I know. Was I wrong?"

"How can I know?"

"How can I?" The little man spread his stubby fingers in a gesture of helplessness. "It's not easy to deal with other men's dreams. Had I the right to tamper with his illusions? Had I a duty to dispel them? I don't know, and you can't tell. Not even he can say whether I should have told him or not. I didn't tell him because I didn't want to hurt him. I'm not a brave man, Matthew. Not like him.

"I like your brother, Matthew. I liked to see him *think*, to see him dream. I liked his *seeking*. It's rare, you know. I didn't want to destroy anything so rare. I didn't want to see it destroyed. But now, if there's any help I can offer, I'd like to be here. I'm sorry."

I sighed. "And what help can you give?" I asked.

"I don't know."

"Can you give him the drug that he needs?"

"I don't know that either."

"There aren't many travellers nowadays," I said.

"Precious few," he agreed. He knew what I was leading up to.

"There aren't many people who know things any more," I continued, "who store knowledge. And there are even fewer with purposes for which that knowledge can be used.

"Yet someone gave a ring to a crippled man. Someone cared. Someone supplies drugs to lonely mountain villages. There are men with their private suns, and men who live at the crossroads of the world. Not much is wasted, is it father? It's a contented world, as we all well know. Happiness is everywhere. Euphoria. But it has to be *helped*, hasn't it father? Tranquility has to be maintained. Someone has to turn the wheels so that the rest of the world might sleep in its feather bed. No one goes hungry, or unfulfilled. We're a childlike people with wonderful toys. Who makes those toys, Brother Álvaro? Who looks after the children?"

"As you know very well," he said quietly, "we do."

"You do," I repeated, in a flat, neutral voice.

"The Brotherhood of the Afterman," he said, equally drily. "We prepare the way. It is the sole purpose left to man on Earth that he should prepare the way for those who will succeed him. We have an aim and a destiny. We do what is necessary."

"Do you have the drug that would enable John to travel in time?"

"We have drugs to extend perception."

"In time?" I persisted.

"Yes."

"And what must we do to buy some of that drug?"

Álvaro shrugged. "It's not for me to say. Come to the Brotherhood, perhaps. Learn from us. Learn with us. Understand us. Let us understand you."

"It's not myself I'm talking about. It's John."

"I don't think there's as much difference as you claim. I mean, between John and yourself."

"He won't join your brotherhood, you know. He doesn't believe in you."

"You don't know your brother, Matthew. He believes. Not necessarily in us, but he believes. It's a start. We need John as much as he needs us. In this age, we are the only committed men. He needs a commitment badly. I think he'll take ours for want of a better one."

"And me? You don't need me."

"John needs you."

"For what? I can't do any more for him. You can. He needs you, if anyone, not me."

Álvaro didn't answer. I looked at my brother's face through the haze which hung lazily around the fire. He did not appear to be listening. I knew that he could close himself off from the world completely if he wanted to, but somehow I felt that his blankness was synthetic—that he had heard every word we said, and was thinking it over. His eyes maintained their constant stare.

"So what do I do?" I asked Álvaro.

He shook his head. "It's not for me to tell you what to do."

"You seemed to be telling me what to do a moment ago."

He smiled. "A point of view. I offer you a way of thinking, not advice. You must decide. You and John."

"John decides," I said.

"Does he really?" The little man's voice was ironic.

"I don't need the illusions. I don't need the missions."

"Perhaps not."

"He leads, and I follow. Someone has to look after him. Even now."

Another pause lengthened into minutes. Álvaro had apparently said his piece, and was now content to let the matter alone. Perhaps he was tired of my perpetually negative attitude. It was, after all, John that he was talking to, not me. It was John that he wanted.

The Firefly still stared into the ebbing flames. There were tears on his cheeks. But I don't believe that he was crying. It was only the smoke getting in his eyes.

PART II

BEYOND TIME'S AEGIS

XII.

ANOTHER SUMMER

The low-walled garden was small. The Brotherhood were economical with their space. They lived in tiny rooms. Their corridors had low ceilings. And their garden seemed cruelly restricted. It was filled with flowers of every color, which had an unimaginable wealth of scent.

It was mid-Summer, and the sky was clear. It had been very hot for a month, and I had been constantly reminded by the sun and the nectar and the humming of bees of the previous summer—the summer John and I had spent roaming the moors and the deserts and the vales and the mountains in search of a man who walked through time.

I found the memories pleasant, but I was beginning to tire of the perpetual eager brightness of the noonday world. I went outside far less often now, preferring the garden with its cloistered surrounds. There was just a touch of coolness here—perhaps more imagined than real—which set off the order and the quietness of the sight and smell of the flowers.

We had come to the Brotherhood just as Autumn began to make travelling uncomfortable and difficult, footsore and weary. I had been very glad of the opportunity for rest. I had remained an honored guest ever since then—performing what seemed to be inadequate labor in return for my keep. John had joined the brothers of the Afterman.

It had surprised me greatly at the time. I had thought that I knew him better than that. But perhaps I never knew him. I began to believe that we had been growing apart ever since he was left in my care as a child. I did not approve of his decision at first. I thought it would make him very un-happy, in the long run. But the change which came over him proved me much mistaken. Contentment he did not find, but calm and confidence he did. His intensity of character re-mained, but it became deeper, and no longer evident in his manner and speech. His anger and his fear lost their hold over him completely. His perpetual emotional torment was soothed into determination.

I was afraid, at first, when the changes were new and so dramatic, that I had lost him forever to the Brotherhood and its ideas. But that did not happen. We were apart for long periods of time while he learned what the humility and phi-losophy of the Afterman doctrine had to teach him, but he always returned to me for something—I don't know what—that the Brotherhood couldn't give him.

The Brothers of the Afterman had things to teach me, too—or rather, I had things that should be learned. I never became a follower, in the sense that I accepted a duty to the Afterman, let alone a Brother to dedicate my life to preparing his way. But I did believe that an Afterman would come. And, of course, I prized the currency in which they dealt with Mankind—peace and contentment, by any means which came to hand.

And so, on that day in mid-Summer, I was still at the monastery, in the cloisters, looking at the garden and waiting for John. Brother John, he was now, not just *my* brother John, who called himself the Firefly.

He approached from behind me, so that I did not see him. He moved quietly, and did not speak until he was be-side me.

"It's late," he said. "I'm sorry."

I shook my head. "There is time. It's only just past noon."

"It's the last day," he said. "The last day of all."

"You're definitely going?"

"*We're* going, Matthew. You must come with us."

"I've not been told that I can go," I pointed out. "I'm no servant of the Afterman. Not a member of the Brotherhood, anyhow. This pilgrimage is a matter of some importance to the people here. It's taken a lot of work and a lot of preparation."

He took my arm in his hand. "There has never been any question about your coming, Matthew. It is not for any of us to say that the journey is only for those who accept the bond. You are my brother, and Joaz and Xavier are my brothers."

"But I'm no brother to Joaz and Xavier. It's not just your pilgrimage, John."

"It's as much mine as the search for the man who walked through time. It's my idea. You came with me then, and you must come with me now."

I was touched by a sudden sadness, and a little fear. I loved this world, this time, the old monastery, its gardens, its surrounds. I'd been happy here. I didn't really want to embark upon a strange mission into the unknowable future.

"What is this pilgrimage *for*?" I asked him, and I could feel the anxiety fraying my voice. "Why, John? You're a different man now from the man who chased dreams of the past a year ago. Why must we leave again, on another quest for another, stranger dream?"

He tugged at my wrist so that I looked him in the eye.

"I'm not a different man," he insisted. "People don't really change inside—only on the surface."

I could see the John of old in his eyes, as though the reflections of the sun in his pupils were distant fireflies.

"Who else?" I asked.

"Only Joaz and Xavier."

"Not Leon? Not even old Álvaro?"

"It's a long journey. We may need a great deal of the elixir. Four is enough. And besides, Leon and Álvaro and all the others belong *here*. This quest will take us far away from the responsibilities of the present. I need to go. So do Joaz and Xavier. So do you. But no one else. In a way, I suppose, we're running...going to see the results of our work instead of *doing* the work." He laughed briefly. "The Brotherhood can't spare too many of us. Only those who *must* go. Most belong here."

I belong here, I said to myself. *Maybe I'm no use. Maybe the Brotherhood is glad to send me and not a valu-*

able member of its organization. But this *world is mine. I belong here.*

"What's the point?" I asked aloud. "There's no way of getting word back to this time, to tell Leon and Álvaro and all the rest that the work has borne fruit, that the plan is a success, that the duty is fulfilled. What does anyone gain, if no one but us can ever know?"

He let go my arm, and a shadow of faint exasperation crossed his face. "You never understood, Matthew," he said, with a hint of sourness. "Perhaps you never will. It's like the old legends of the quest for the Holy Grail. It is for some simply to know of it, some to work for it, some to prepare for its coming, and for some very few to see it and touch it.

"That *one* of us sees—that is enough for all. Can't you understand that? Can't you understand that when Joaz and Xavier and you and I take the drug and walk through the centuries, that we will be carrying with us the hopes and the blessings of hundreds of men—thousands more in the past and the future. If *one* of us can see, if one of us can *know*, the emergence and triumph of the Afterman, then that will be enough."

"But how does everyone else know what we feel? How can they ever be sure that we'll succeed? For all they know we may be taking a journey into nowhere, to find nothing but ultimate oblivion."

"Oh, Matthew," he sighed. "They know. They know *now*, they really do. Because they have faith."

"I don't believe in faith," I said.

"Because *you* have none," he replied, "must you deny it to others as well?" I was shocked then, momentarily. A year ago, John would never have said that.

He would commit himself to a truth or deny it. It was I who had always preached the doctrine of letting others believe what they wished. Had I, I wondered, changed for the worse while he grew wiser?

"There's been too much talk," I said. "Too much talk and nothing shown. I'm growing old, John. I never had dreams like yours. I think you'd better go without me."

I said that reluctantly, but I had to say it. Just in case he wanted me to go solely because I was his brother. To give him the chance to forget me and follow his dream, if that was what he really wanted.

"We'll go together," he said fiercely. "We *must*. To the end of time. You and I will both see the Afterman. I *know* it."

There was a brief silence.

"*I know it*," he whispered again.

XIII.

THE LAST DAY

For most of my year at the monastery, I had worked in the laboratories where Leon distilled all kinds of drugs and medicines from all manner of vegetable substances.

Brother Leon was a strong, thoughtful man with a propensity for work that often seemed unhealthy. I rarely entered his rooms without finding him somewhere within, tending to one or another of his hundreds of growing cultures, or running some extraction apparatus. He had uncommonly large hands, and it always amazed me to watch them at work, for they were not in the least awkward. Though he spent hour after hour with fragile, and precious, glassware, I never once saw him break a piece.

He explained to me the processes by which the strange chemical substances were produced.

"A great many plants produce odd chemical compounds in small quantities, which are, so far as I can tell, not in the least useful to the plants. Poisons like curare, stimulants like digitalis, hallucinogens like lysergic acid, and alkaloids like atropine. For many years, doctors searched out these compounds, selected out plants that would produce specific ones. We've continued their work. We inherited most of their knowledge and a lot of their specialized strains. Practically all the important work—the testing and the classifying—was done well before our time. We've refined techniques a little, found one or two agents unknown a few centuries ago. But our work has been principally directed to the *use* of the drugs, their purpose within our philosophy, and their dispensation. We can kill, we can heal. We can make dreams and emotions. We can cure illness and alleviate pain. We can bring sleep and destroy misery. And we can alter perception to the extent where we can move time itself around us.

"Our purposes are simple. We aim to preserve the race of Man, but only so that he may give birth to the Afterman. We are concerned with the quality of human life, but only as a secondary consideration. The Afterlife is the important thing. We have been accused of bringing senility to the human race, but we believe that it is more maturity than old age. We believe that the age of struggle and ambition was only a childhood. It is pleasant, perhaps, to remember in stories and legends, but it is behind us now. We have put away childish things. We look forward, not outward.

"There are others who say that our ways are cruel. That selling dreams in favor of realities is dealing in false currency, cheating men of the true happiness which they might otherwise gain had they the opportunity to pursue it. Perhaps so, but I cannot think of it as cruel to bring peace. Not *cruel*. It would have been very wrong, I think, for our forbears to allow the race of Man to die in wretched despair, tearing itself to pieces in its frenetic struggle to excel beyond its capabilities. The Afterman must not be denied a chance of life because Man cannot be the lord of the universe. Do you agree?"

I had, to a certain extent. I would never commit myself to so strong a belief, excluding more simple ways of thought, but I always found Leon far more convincing than the philosophical, talkative Álvaro.

Leon was sorry when I told him that I was leaving, but not in the least surprised. The proposed pilgrimage had been in the air a long time, and I think everyone had known that, in the end, I would go with my brother.

"I wish you the best of luck," said Leon.

"Thank you," I replied, in a somewhat lukewarm fashion. We stood before one of Leon's beloved glass cages, in which grew the most prized of all his treasures. It looked rather ugly, and not at all suited to the great role that its distillate was to perform. It was a fungus, consisting of a vast network of hyphae stitching a mass of humus, dead leaves, black soil and mucus into a large dirty disc. The fruiting bodies, from which the time drug was actually extracted, were mushrooms with short stalks and massive, bulbous heads. The heads were gray-brown in color; the outer skin was perpetually peeling away, turning dull purple as the tissues died and desiccated.

"It's a funny business," said Leon, opening the cage and reaching in with gloved hands to remove five or six of the mushrooms. "They grow so fast, yet we get so little elixir from such a lot of tissue. It's taken years to distill our current supply of serum, despite their wildfire growing. They'll eat anything, so long as it's dead."

"Is it dangerous?" I asked. "The drug, I mean."

He separated the heads neatly from the stalks, and began to pulp them in a wooden bowl with practiced twirls of a club-like pestle.

"Don't really know," he replied. "Was a difficult one to test, you see. All that's written about it tends to be a mite speculative. I mean, give it to a man and he's gone—weeks or years displaced in time. Made experimental tabulation a little difficult. They never really managed to work out a consistent dosage ratio, either. Varies a lot from person to person.

"But I don't think you need worry. The ones who came through all seemed healthy. We even get a few these days like your friend. A lot of them go on, too, so there's likely even more just pass through."

"Pass through. You mean they don't even register in this time?"

"Probably don't even notice it. It's all a matter of perception, remember. What the eye doesn't see, the body doesn't bother about. Oh, I suppose they must *be* here, somehow. But I wouldn't recognize one. Not unless he stopped to talk to me."

"And what then? When they do stop?"

"They appear, and they disappear. No pattern to the time they spend, from what I've gleaned from other people's stories. They seem to be perfectly ordinary people. No evidnt derangement of their subjective time sense. The drug seems to affect the universe more than it does them. That's a distortion, of course. Only a matter of their point of view."

"How far do you think we'll be able to go?" I asked.

"To the end, I hope. As I said, we don't know much about dosage. But there should be enough in the flasks by now to take you a billion years or more, if necessary. Even that's not far, I suppose. The Earth's a lot older than that. But if I had to guess, I'd say it'll take you as far as you want to go. Or need to go."

"I'm not sure how far that is," I confessed.

"You'll know soon."

"I wonder what it's like," I said. "That's something I never asked the man who walked through time. I never thought, I suppose, that one day I'd be doing the same thing. I suppose you just move from time to time, as if you were looking at different things, and not studying everything that lies in between with the same attention. We see so little of what's before our eyes, I suppose."

He grinned at me, all the while grinding the gray mess in his bowl with a constant, determined motion of his wrist. "It'll be just like that," he confirmed.

Since I'd based my analogy on his words, it wasn't surprising that he agreed.

"Just like walking through history—future history, that is. Moving on to something new, pausing to look in detail, passing everything but without the need or the capacity to observe everything. You'll have to hurry, you know. Can't stop to stare. You've only one lifetime to travel to the end of time. But I suppose that brother of yours won't let you rest. He's not the sort of man to let time slip by unused."

"No," I said. "He'll want to be away again the instant we've stopped. No rest, no chance to learn and understand. He's always been that way."

Leon put the bowl down with a sudden snap, and peeled the tight gloves from his fingers. His eyes were already searching for the distilling apparatus. I still wanted to talk, to make the most of these last few hours in the safety and security of what I knew. But Leon was busy making just a little last drop of the drug—the last drop which might just conceivably give us the one glimpse of the Afterman. He didn't want to be bothered any more.

John and Joaz and Xavier were preparing themselves in private. I didn't know where to find Álvaro. Those were the only people I knew well enough to talk to on this, the most important of days.

So I went out into the garden again, and wandered in and out of the cloisters, tasting the fragrant air, savoring the sunlight as though it was the last time I'd ever see the sun.

I knelt down and felt the soil, picked grass and touched it with the tip of my tongue. I listened to the sound of buzzing flies and whining grasshoppers. Mere hours before, these sounds had seemed irritating. Now, I wanted to hear them until I was certain that I knew them perfectly.

I left the monastery buildings, and went wandering along the hill paths, doing nothing but experiencing the world that I had taken for granted during the thirty-four years previous to this day.

The last whole, long day of all.

I had no doubt that I was behaving like a common fool. Tomorrow would contain the same things as today. Except that it would not be *tomorrow*, but a composite of a hundred tomorrows, separated by I knew not how much of a lapse in time.

How fast does one walk through time? I wondered.

Can one run or saunter?

How do we find one another if we're separated?

Was actual movement in space implicit in movement in time, or could I sit perfectly still and watch the world change around me?

It was new, so very new. And I, so old and set in my ways and contented.

Not like little John, a mere twenty years old, still full of youth.

I did not want to go. But I had to.

XIV.

PILGRIMAGE

It was a beginning of cosmic proportions—grand and splendid. But I was tired of beginnings and the awe of the cosmos. I had seen them all before, in my dreams, induced by the drug that permeated my body and blood.

I was certain, then, that what we were searching for was an illusion. We sought answers, we looked for conclusions and consummations. We looked for everything to fall into place like pieces in a jigsaw, to bring order and roundness to what we knew and believed.

But after that beginning—the beginning of time itself—I was certain that there could be no neatness, no roundness, no order to be brought forth from this chaos.

At first, the sequence blinded me. It took time to adjust Time, for my senses to cope with the new manner of flow which attacked them. I realized, very slowly, that what I was seeing was not the future at all, but the past. At an incredible pace, millions of years to a single instant, the pages flew and flickered.

The very ground beneath my feet writhed and moved and changed its shape. Days and nights fled so quickly that there was only the barest flicker to show that day was not eternal. The sun's path was a glaring rainbow stretching from horizon to horizon and moving rapidly back and forth across the sky as seasons were gone before they could be noticed. The only physical sensation of which I was aware was a bitter cold wind, which seemed to blow through and through me. It was not a real wind, but I could not guess what it might be. There was not the slightest sign of John or Joaz or Xavier.

Life began. I did not see it, of course. I regretted that such an event should pass by while I could guess that it was happening, yet leaving me unable to detect it. It was not the work of a moment, even at this breathless rush, but all I could see was turbid water, and that a long way off. All that lay around me was an expanse of desolate rock. Lifeless, yet moving. Forever shifting and quaking. I watched the mountains gather themselves, only to be smashed down again by the surge of the ages. But I could not watch the molecules forming and reforming, growing and replicating. Tiny, barely tangible colloids finding the secrets of immortality and metamorphosis.

I waited, alone, as far as I could tell.

I saw the world as a god might have seen it. But I was no god, because I was impotent, and no god may be impotent if he is to have meaning outside himself.

I had no alternative but to learn humility, and know that although Fate might not be an active, vital force, it was a state of mind which accurately conceived the manner of real events. In a few seconds, I was granted a vast range of experience without yielding the transience which could lend significance to my environment. What I saw *meant* something, for all that I could see hardly anything at all.

Later—I don't know how much later—there were living things I could see. I met the fragile glasslike organisms which lived in the streams and pools that occasionally flowed past me or formed beside me and around me. I seemed often to be standing on water rather than on earth, and sometimes on air as the ground shifted, but my position never seemed precarious. I was fixed, and time flew about me.

There were armored creatures then, with hard, spiraled shells or spicules or thick, indented plates. But they still seemed fragile, somehow, as though the living parts were hiding in a cocoon from the least disturbance.

I never quite accustomed myself to the presence of life and all it involved—the flux and continuity, the ceaseless change. I saw the life at first as a rush—a ceaseless chaos of competition and hope and extinction. But I soon perceived a different pattern—a deep, constant image behind the superficial turbulence.

There was something in life, I saw, that was sedate and calm. Something that knew where it was going and picked its way carefully—an unruffled conqueror moving with self-assured strategy in its advance, trailing multitudinous excretions in its wake. Just one thread, though somehow a part and function of the whole. The mainstream of evolution.

The land was invaded. By this time, the seas were completely conquered. The primary producers moved quietly and unhurriedly out of the comfortable womb into the harsh world of air and rock. And where the plants went, the animals followed. As soon as a way of life was made ready for them on land, they began to leave the sea.

But still, for a long time, the powerhouse of life remained in the sea. Life on land was too hard, too difficult to permit flexibility in the creatures who lived there. For a long time—perhaps a minute or more, subjectively—everything that was new came out of the sea. Only when there were a thousand different components in the land-based life-system did it begin to move of its own accord, directionally. The nematode worms came out of the sea. The arthropods came out of the sea. And, eventually, the fish came out of the sea. The jawless, armored osteolepid fish climbed out on to the land and carried the mainstream of life to its new environment.

And so on, building now with a comfortable precision that was always clear and visible, not blurred and hidden.

I was fully adjusted now to this mode of perception. I think that about four or five hours of subjective time had passed. I had no difficulty now in seeing things whose individual lifespans could be measured only in nanoseconds built up a collective image, rather in my brain than in my eye, and they registered, presenting themselves for contemplation.

I came to know intimately the philosophy of life. I made no attempt to deify life, or attribute any mystic or magical quality to it. I describe it as a "philosophy" because it was directional. It had an aim. It did not merely exist. It was a process and not a property. Its aim was order. The total possession of the entire universe. Its clear intent was to subvert the entropic principle and bring order to the whole of existence.

Great forests of seed-ferns and calamites consumed the empty ground, fixing sunbeams into energy and building bodies out of air and water. The land-snails and the insects were everywhere, but in terms of the main line, it was the day of the reptiles. They surged in several directions at once—back to the seas as turtles and ichthyosaurians; into the treetops as archaeopteryx, the first bird-reptile. The sheer size of the dinosaurs was impressive, but they were not main-liners. By the time they reached their full size and development, it was already the twilight of the reptilian age. The mammals were coming. The reptiles had invented the cleidoic egg. The mammals invented homiothermy. The dinosaurs, without adequate control over their body temperature, pressed by size selection into allometric growth traps, perished very easily. But they made their impression upon me. I remembered the lethargic stegosaur, with its incomparable armor, and the vicious, slaughtering allosaur long after I forgot the bird-limbed miniature dragons that gave rise to the mammals. Most of all, I treasured the memory of the brontosaur. No one could imagine the pathos of its hopeless majesty as it lived briefly and faded away, bewildered by its own size and feebleness.

The mammals seemed like vermin while their distant cousins still lived, but the small insect-eaters were the meek who inherited the Earth. Man was but a breath and a half away now. The sequence was virtually complete. Once I had realized this, I felt a wave of relief. With only a few seconds to go, I once again gave time to anticipate instead of retrospect.

While the uintatheria and megatheria stalked around me, I relaxed for the first time since I had drunk the elixir. The dawn horses came, and the wolf and the hippopotamus, but I was wondering now whether the whole thing was a dream, or whether Leon and the man who walked through time had been wrong, and the past could be reached after all.

I began to look out for the main line again, for Man and the ancestors of Man. I saw the mastodon and the woolly rhinoceros and the saber-toothed tiger.

But no Man. He was insignificant. He hid among the trees. I might have caught a glimpse had I stared really hard. But there was too much else to see that my attention was forever compelled to wander.

I thought, briefly, that if John were here somewhere, then *he* would see Man. *He* would not be distracted.

And then it was finished. All of history went by in a handful of microseconds. I did see it, I think, but only as a fleeting image, the most ephemeral of illusions.

John touched me on the shoulder.

"I think I was dreaming," I said.

"No," said Joaz. "It wasn't a dream. It was a vision. A true vision. We *saw* it, with our eyes." Joaz was a tall, spectral man with dark eyes and a thin, penetrative voice.

"But we can only go forward in time," I persisted.

"We can't *go*," said John, and I knew there was regret in his voice for the past that contained his Golden Age lasted so much less than a moment that we had not been able to see it. "But we *saw*. It's behind us. Fixed and unreachable. But it's there. It's real. We could look at it, and we did. But so *much*. And so quickly."

"Where are we?" complained Xavier. He was short and stout, with a perpetual tremble in his voice that was not really fear at all. He was, above all else, a *kind* man. A man who would cry for another man's troubles and berate himself for his own.

I looked around. It was dark, but there were stars to see by. The sane, still stars. We stood upon the same hills, our sandaled feet crushing the same grass. I searched the dimness for the monastery.

"See," said Xavier, pointing. "It's still here. We haven't moved at all. The drug has failed."

"It's not the same," said John quietly. He was confident, taking charge. It was, after all, *his* quest, *his* mission. "It's deserted, Xavier. Perhaps even a ruin. No lights, Brother. No lights."

"But they wouldn't leave it!" protested Xavier.

"Not," said Joaz ambivalently, "in a hundred years."

We stood then, in contemplation. We had walked through time. Yesterday was gone. Forever. The silence lasted for a long time.

Then John—it *had* to be John—broke out into laughter. "We're *here*," he said. "We're *going*. Come on, Matthew, take my hand. Let's all join hands and *walk. Walk!*"

It was the first time in many years that I'd seen him exultant, full of joy. He jostled our elbows and pushed us, all three at once. And we responded, having no will left to resist.

We walked.

We walked on and on, and time flowed around us, faster and faster and faster.

XV.

THE DANCE

We paused on the side of a long, shallow hill. We were very tired. We had walked too far, perhaps expecting, illogically, that because the passage of time was now ours to command, we would need no rest, no sleep. Night and day might pass at the whim of our footsteps, but the metabolic clocks inside us still kept their own perfect time.

The grass was dark and coarse. It was late evening, and the weather was damp and misty. The scene was somber and almost despondent, as though painted in dim, uncertain water-colors.

"This is no place to stay the night," Joaz pointed out. "We'll have to go on a little further, at least."

"I can't go another step," said Xavier definitely. "Here we've stopped, and here I intend to stay for ten minutes."

"Tomorrow might be a lot better, and it can't be far," I put in.

"Can you be so sure of reaching tomorrow?" Xavier wanted to know. "I've been trying to stop for the last hour, every time I saw somewhere worth stopping. But my judgment just isn't that refined yet. Maybe with practice, we can pick our spots exactly. But at this moment, *now*, I need a rest."

John had listened to the conversation in unsmiling silence. He said nothing, apparently content to wait.

"We seem to be linked together somehow," said Joaz. "That's why we have difficulty stopping at any one place. We all have to be concentrating on the same spot."

"How can we be linked together?" I wanted to know.

Joaz shrugged. "I'm not sure. State of mind, I suppose. We regard ourselves as being together, we stay together. The travel in time, when all said and done, is only a matter of personal perception. And what we think conditions at least *the way* we see, if not what we see."

I could not be bothered to try to see what he was getting at. I was content not to understand. This constant metaphysical dialogue was wearing me down. What did it matter *why* we stayed together, as long as we *did*. That surely was the only point of importance. As long as none of us found himself alone, stranded, with no way of getting back to his companions.

I extended a foot tentatively, half afraid that I might slip through time, although both Joaz and John had been moving about quite freely. Then, encouraged, I walked a short distance up the slope. "Will it be all right if I go up and look round," I asked, "while there's still light?"

I addressed the question to Joaz, who seemed most at ease, but it was John who answered. "A few minutes," he said. "No more. And stay in sight."

I wandered up the slope toward the brow of the hill, hurrying to get there before the twilight faded away.

As I came to the crown, I saw two figures on the other slope, immobile except for the gentle movements of their clothes in the wind. I hesitated, wondering whether to call the others to take a look. But a glance back assured me that neither Xavier nor John would be interested, and Joaz was facing the other way. I turned back to watch, standing still rather than approaching, for I was somewhat breathless.

They were both staring intently at something which I could not see, not because it was hidden but because it simply wasn't there. They did not talk...merely stared. They were facing a direction almost directly opposite to mine, and obviously could not see me.

After a moment or so, a rainbow haze began to rise slowly and unevenly from the damp grass. It crept slowly, like a living smoke, careless of the wind. They had apparently been waiting for this, for it rose from the spot at which they stared.

106

Very slowly, the rainbow arranged itself into a bower of vivid colors.

I could not imagine what kind of substance it could be. It seemed to be drawing energy from somewhere—whether from the air or from the ground I could not tell—and began to expand smoothly until it was about six feet in height. Then it stopped growing and began to spin on its vertical axis. There was still no definite shape discernible, although the rotation gradually enforced a discoid distribution upon the particles—if there were particles.

Without ceasing to spin, the colored air began to dance. Gyrating smoothly and rhythmically, it conveyed the impression of music.

One of the figures, to whom I had paid little attention so far, was a woman dressed in black lace. She was standing absolutely still, cold and unreachable, watching the colored mist but apparently unmoved by it. I could not see her eyes, but her shoulders were thrown back proudly, her head inclined slightly upward, as though she were trying to look *down* upon the dancing light. Her hands hung limply by her sides. Her whole manner seemed somehow aristocratic.

The second figure was a man, standing a little way behind the woman. His hands were folded across his chest. He was shorter than she, and dressed entirely in black. I could not make out whether he was a companion, a servant or a guard.

I began to move round a little way, trying to get a better view of the couple, but I remembered the injunction about not going out of sight. I glanced back. Joaz was slowly ascending the hill behind me. I caught his eye and beckoned to him. He nodded, but did not quicken his pace.

The rainbow disc changed shape, elongating and rounding off gently, then wavering and quivering into a more complex form. I watched closely, trying to make out the intricacies of the new shape. It was vaguely humanoid, but the ever-whirling colors made it very difficult to make out any fine features.

Joaz arrived by my side, took in the entire scene with one sweep of his blue-black eyes and glanced sideways at me.

"What is it?" he asked.

"It came out of the ground. They were waiting for it. I don't know why."

He returned his eyes to the dancer, which was moving more slowly now, its colors *reaching out* somehow, plucking at something in my mind.

"It's hurting me," I said, and found that I could not take my eyes off the thing. I felt a sudden wave of fear, and began to fancy that it was taunting me—that there was something obscene in the way it moved. I knew that Joaz, too, was fascinated by the thing. I felt rather than saw or heard his stillness.

"It's hurting," I repeated, glad that I could speak, at least.

"It's hurting her, too," he said, without emotion.

It was as though a battle had been joined. The woman's hands had closed upon themselves into tight fists which squeezed and squeezed. As her dress was held against her by the wind, I could see the knotted muscles of her back rigid beneath the thin material.

Darkness was falling quickly, and the living light was now the only illumination of any magnitude. The stars were hidden by thick cloud. I knew that John and Xavier must be aware of the light by now, but I could not hear them. I wished that I could turn and look to see if they were coming up the slope.

The rhythm of the dance began to accelerate again.

I felt my mouth being forced into a tight, grim line, but it was as if the colors themselves were doing it, and not my own muscles. My skin felt as if it were tingling with coldness, and my eyeballs felt like globes of ice.

It seemed, somehow, that the colors were taking heat from my body. I felt a hand on my shoulder, a hand which, gently but firmly, pulled my head round. I made no resistance. My line of vision swung away from the light, and I stared into John's face.

My head buzzed as the sensations all died away.

"Don't look at it again," he said. But he was looking over my shoulder. He was watching it. I tried to put my hand in front of his eyes, and he looked me full in the face, then pulled my hand away.

"It's all right," he said. "It won't hurt me."

"What is it?" I asked.

"A swarm of flies."

"Fireflies!" I laughed, hysterically—a short, angry bark.

"I don't know," he said. "Not like those I've seen."

I wondered how he knew. "Can you see them?" I asked. "Each one, not just the whole?"

"Yes," he replied, nodding.

I sneaked a sideways glance at Joaz. He was still staring, still apparently petrified. Xavier stood beside him, shielding his eyes with his palm, peeping out every now and then between the fingers. I reached out to pluck at Joaz's sleeve.

"He's all right," John assured me.

"I want to look," I said.

"Well, shield your eyes," he replied.

I put my palm over my face and turned back. The burning figure was moving slowly over the heath now, approaching the two humans with deliberate steps which looked, to me, menacing. Flimsy fire-feathers and brief flares shot away and rejoined the mass as it moved unevenly. Now that I knew what it was, I began to make out the individual lights. They were, indeed, only fireflies.

The woman's hands half-raised themselves, her fists unclenching once as she tried to wave the flies back. But the colored swarm merely swayed and eddied, and she missed them. Then the rainbow enveloped her, and her companion also. But while he stood stock still, haloed by shifting color, she turned and ran.

I saw her face then, blanched white and fearful. Her eyes were like chips of ice, sparkling in the light reflected from the flies. She fell to the ground, her long dress tripping her up.

The colors swayed above her prostrate form, and then drifted off, fading and winking out, one by one. The others had left the man, also. As the darkness came, he was moving across to help the woman. Neither seemed in any way injured. I lost them in the blackness of night just as he leaned over to pick her up.

I reached out a hand, fearfully, to touch John. His hand met mine, and held it firmly.

"What happened?" I demanded.

"They fed, I think."

"On what? Blood?"

"I don't think so." His voice sounded strange and distant. I could hardly see him.

"It hurt me to look at them, at first," I confessed.

"It wasn't pain," he said. "They were holding your mind. That's all. Just holding it."

"But why?"

"I don't know."

"How do you come to know so much, yet know nothing at all?" I demanded, annoyed by his calmness.

"I don't know," he said again, his voice still uncharged with any emotion.

"Joaz!" I appealed. "What is happening? Have we all gone mad?"

"No," he said. "Keep a hold on yourself, Matthew. I think it's the drug."

"Hallucinations, you mean?"

"Oh, no. It's real. But the drug is refining our perception as well as spreading it along the timeline. We can all see more, know more. *Depth* of perception as well as *length*. Perhaps strength too."

"But why can you see, and not me?" I wanted to know.

"We're adjusting more quickly. It takes time, Matthew."

I shook my head. The darkness all around me began to frighten me again. "Let's go," I said. "To daylight. Anywhere, away from here."

"All right," said John, and he kept hold of my hand as the darkness fell away behind us, and I could see again.

But I didn't want to see. I just wanted to know that I could. I was very tired, and I only wanted to sleep. My head felt strange and heavy. I became conscious of the fact that I was leaning on John, and that he was supporting me with both arms.

"It's all right," he said. "It's only a matter of time. You'll understand, in time. It's a matter of adaptation. We'll sleep soon."

110

I don't remember going to sleep. I don't remember our stopping again. But I remember that when I awoke, I still didn't know what had happened on that hillside—to the man and the woman, or to me.

I was only just beginning to realize that the future was an alien place. A horribly strange place that might, eventually, dissolve into a chaos completely beyond my comprehension.

I was consumed with fear. But there was John by my side—John, who was ready and eager for anything new. Who *wanted* to find alien worlds and new conceptions.

I had always needed John.

And, it seemed, I always would.

XVI.

THE UNICORN

Vegetation spread around us in a thick tangle of green and brown. Sleek, supple branches cascaded from tree trunks, brushing the ground with their tips, and twining around one another into aerial arches, matted braids and hives of dusky green. Long grass grew everywhere the trunks did not, reaching up to the branches and enveloping the lowest of the leaves.

We stopped in a small clearing carpeted by dark green moss and fanlike ferns sprouting like massive leaves from the ground. Under the moss were loose flat stones, which explained the absence of grass and trees. Between the stones squatted fungal clumps, and similar growths fed on dead and dying trees.

Moisture dragged painfully along the tendrils in tiny drops, and the cracked bark of the trees ran rivulets of water down to the sodden ground. The whole forest around us had been drenched by a recent heavy rainfall.

We did not sit down, but paused to look around.

"There was something built here once," commented Xavier.

"Precious little of it left now," said Joaz. "Probably overgrown even in our time."

"How long ago was that?" I asked. "How far do you think we've come?"

"I don't know," Joaz replied.

"Does it matter?" asked John.

"I thought I'd like to know," I said, uncomfortably. They seemed to have adjusted so fast...even slow, amiable Xavier. They saw more than I, they had a pattern ready made in their minds into which they fitted every new experience. I didn't know what it was that I lacked, but I knew that all three of them were in possession of some faculty which I had not, as yet, discovered. Nothing startled them. Nothing frightened them. They asked no questions, yet knew so very few answers. I had thought that our vision of the past had taught me a great deal. But apparently, it had not taught me enough.

Of course, there remained the fact that all three of them had *needed* to undertake this mission. It had been a part of them long before they even started. But it was not my need, it was not my mission. I was a passenger. Perhaps I had no right to understand.

"There are no insects," I said.

"It's wet," Xavier pointed out. "You wouldn't expect to see them."

"But not even on the tree trunks. And the air's clear, but nothing flies."

"Well," said Xavier reasonably, "I doubt that the insects have become extinct since we last stopped."

I continued my inspection. John was talking to Joaz in a low voice. I could have heard what they were saying had I paused to listen, but I did not bother.

Despite the dampness and the monotony of the coloring, the place seemed to me to be very beautiful. Little wraiths of vapor rose from the ground in the hot air, blurring the wall of green just enough to destroy its harshness. It was very quiet, save for the faint sound of water dripping into the grass. There was no wind to rustle the branches, no animal to stir them.

And yet something moved.

I caught only a half-glimpse, in the corner of my eye, but it was enough to turn me in my path and chase it. I did not know what it might be that moved so silently within the thicket, but I was sure that it was real, and not some play of the multitudinous shadows.

As I moved clumsily towards the place where I had seen the movement, I put the creature to fright, and it fled, pausing only once to look at me.

It was a small, slender animal, with the shape of a horse but the size of a hare. Its fur was bronze atop its back, fading to ermine whiteness at the belly. Its mane was long and silvery, its eyes bright and coppery red. Its tail was like a flicker of silver flame, tossing and shaking as it moved swiftly away without moving a single one of the hanging leaf-clad strands.

I saw it so briefly as it bounded away into the impassable wall of greenery but of one thing I am sure: between the creature's sharp ears rose a slender, curling helix of pearly horn. It shone with the brilliance of sunlight reflected from its mirror-smooth surface.

It was a unicorn. But if this was the unicorn of the legends I had heard in my youth, then the myths had forgotten all but the merest shadow of its reality.

I turned away reluctantly, knowing that I could not follow, and returned to my companions.

"I saw a unicorn," I said, halfheartedly. I did not know whether to expect ridicule or total indifference.

"Where was it?" asked John.

"In the forest."

"You're sure?" This from Joaz.

"I'm sure."

Their eyes scanned the trees around us. There was no sound, no sign of any movement. I could see that Joaz and Xavier neither believed nor disbelieved. John alone knew that I had seen what I had seen. He knew me well enough to judge my voice.

"How can a legend of the past become a reality of the future?" I asked.

John studied me carefully. "You're different here," he commented. "Back at the monastery, in the mountain, even years before that, you never asked questions. You already knew all the answers that you cared about. Here, you're forever looking around for something new, forever demanding explanations."

114

It was true. I liked to know where I was and what I was about. I had been comfortable in my own time. I had known the world, and what it contained. I never had need to be surprised, or change my ideas. I had not been this way since I was a small child.

"That doesn't answer my question," I pointed out.

"There are a great number of realities, Matthew," said Joaz. "In time, perhaps, all dreams can come true."

"But there hasn't *been* time," I pointed out. "We've hardly moved over the last few days, compared to what we saw during those first hours, when the past flowed through us. And even at that pace, life moved slowly."

"Life did," said Joaz. "But not Man. The life of Man was invisible. We don't know, Matthew, that the ages we saw in a few hours passed any more quickly than the minutes do now, when we think time travels at its normal pace. Time isn't constant in its passage. Haven't you seen that? We can't say of *now* that we are a specific distance from when we started, nor that the beginning of time was so much beyond that. Time isn't distance, Matthew. It's *not* a dimension, a measure, a fixed quantity. It's a new perception altogether. Aren't you able to use your eyes and *see* that?"

"No," I confessed. "I'm not. I can't see at all. To me, it's nothing but confusion and bewilderment."

"Poor Matthew," interposed John. "To look so hard and see so little."

He smiled ironically. I felt suddenly that I was a child, and he the adult smiling upon me from his lofty heights of experience and self-confidence. Was this how I had appeared to him when he was younger?

"I wish I'd never come," I said.

A sacrilegious thing to say. It made John instantly sad. I knew he felt responsible for my being here. I knew, too, that he wanted me here, by his side, when he fulfilled his dream. If his dream could ever be fulfilled.

"I'm sorry," I said. "I didn't mean that. But it's all so strange. You've changed so much that you're beyond me. I can't ever understand. I'm misplaced. It's not my kind of a world. I'm a burden to you."

"No," said John. "Never a burden. A source of strength. We all need someone to lean on, Matthew. The more we *need*, the more we need to lean. This quest can't succeed without you. Perhaps, in the end, it will be your eyes we need to tell us when we have succeeded, and not ours. We see different things, but that only means that together we see more."

He was sincere. I wished that I could believe him. But I knew that it was from *him* that I had always drawn *my* strength. Was it possible that two people could draw what they needed from each other? Where, in the end, did all the strength come from?

I couldn't answer. They weren't my sort of problems. I wasn't a thinker, not in the way that Joaz and Álvaro were. I was an ordinary, peaceful man, who *lived* his life instead of trying to find it.

Once, John had been lost in my world. Now, I was lost in his.

XVII.

OTHER LANDS, OTHER LORDS

The sun was a crimson orb in the western sky. A streak of pink and purple cloud lay unmoving beneath it, like a cushion upon which it rested. To the shadowy east were other sprays of cloud, emerging from the mountains like blossoming flowers. Up above, the sky was clearer, broken only by the scarred silver face of the moon, which hung at the zenith. It was a grossly swollen moon, exhibiting far more detail of its age-unaltered surface to the naked eye. The smiling man and the old lady with her bundle of sticks that I used to see there in my youth were no longer evident. Although the features of the satellite were the same, its closeness now gave the illusion of serpentine Chinese dragons wrestling with shadowed, blue-cowled figures like monks.

"It's not at all what I expected," complained Brother Xavier, mopping away the sweat that trickled down his cheeks. The journey was beginning to take a heavy toll of Xavier. He was not in the best of health, and he was beginning to sound both frightened and reluctant. I had become a little more settled as he had grown worse, and I was in a position now to feel sorry for him.

"Other lands," said Brother Joaz, as though that sufficed as an explanation. John made no comment at all. Both of them were suffering in their fashion from the heat, but not nearly so badly as the rotund Xavier.

"Perhaps illusion, perhaps not," I commented. "It won't last forever. There must be something beyond, something outside."

Xavier was silent, sparing his hoarse breath for walking. He seemed not in the least reassured. His friendly, generous face was strained and contorted, but he did not ask to rest. We had already stopped once in this forsaken land which seemed to stretch forever in time and space.

Even under the twin lanterns of sun and moon, the Earth was but feebly lighted. The sun was very dim, and the moon, despite its nearness, somehow less distinct and redder in complexion. A third sprinkle of light fell like a gentle, powdery snowstorm from a shimmering aurora which hung like ribboned hair above the southern horizon. There was no cloud around this, but the sky was stained red and brown as though by aerial dust or by refraction and reflection in the upper layers of the atmosphere.

The ground upon which we walked was dark, broken by waxy crystalline lumps, which were treacherous to traverse, and which hurt my eyes if I looked at them directly for too long. I was unable to decide whether it was reflected light or some property of the weird rock that caused the effect. Great mountains of apparently similar composition ringed the horizon in irregular clumps and jagged ridges. Even the distant mountains glowed like snowglare, but the light was easily tolerable at such a vast distance. They were like the conical stumps of melted candles, all their edges rounded off as though smoothed by fierce heat. Trickles of their fused substance had solidified again while streaming down their slopes and away across the red-black plain.

The rest of the flat ground was lava black, with occasional interspersions of frosty white crust. Such areas, we knew from having crossed them, were hard but brittle, giving way under the feet and making our passage even more difficult. The texture of the white stuff suggested salt, but I formed the impression that it was some kind of ash.

The barrenness and desolation was far worse than anything we had encountered heretofore, and we hated every minute of it, although I was occasionally struck by formations of particular beauty and even an odd kind of nostalgia. Mostly, though, the landscape was simply lonely.

"I can't understand what caused all this," said Xavier eventually. "I didn't see anything. Did you?"

"Not a thing," I replied. "We arrived too fast."

The other two were more reluctant to confess that their omniscience and total understanding could have been so much at fault.

"I don't know what happened," confessed Joaz, "but it lies between us and our destiny. We must either escape through time, or cross it in space."

"It can't go on forever," John added.

Xavier sank gratefully down as John, after his comment, pulled Joaz back from his purposeful stride to rest awhile.

"Don't stop too long on my account," said Xavier, not really meaning it.

"It's all right," said John. "We're all tired. We need the rest."

"I'm slowing you down."

"No, I don't think so. We'll come out of this soon. There's no need to panic."

"I don't like it either," I confessed. "I don't know what it is. I'm afraid of it."

"I know," said John. "We're all afraid. But we must cross it, and cross it we will, one way or another. Have faith."

I muttered some words, which conveyed my own opinion of faith, but I knew that it meant something to both Joaz and Xavier, and I did not want them to hear. I turned my back on them so that they did not see the scowl that crossed my face, and surveyed the scene.

It was as if a teardrop on the Earth's great eyeball had frozen. A great vitreous whirlpool had suddenly come to a halt about a mile away, slightly lower than our present position. It seemed to have stopped dead as if time had been completely and abruptly lost while it was in mid-swirl. A river of gray ice which led to the thing had stopped its onward and downward progress in a frozen leap, its waves breaking into static white spray. It disappeared into hidden spirals of rock at the edge of the round lake. Immediately in front of us, another "river" wandered outward and away over the siliceous skin of the plain. The gray of its ice-water was flecked along its length as far as I could see with blue and gold. Some distance away, it split into hundreds of slender

119

rivulets, each with its own satiny silver sheen, and banks of rust-brown and the deeper black of wood-ash.

And all so still. Full of the promise of life, without the slightest hint of fulfillment.

Frozen still as it was, ripples caught and held, the river seemed to present an impassible barrier to our tired progress. To keep our balance on such a surface in our smooth-soled sandals would be all but impossible. But cross it, it seemed, we had to. I knew that it would not be as fearsome as it appeared to be at a distance. It would be far more substantial. Only at this range was the illusion that we would be walking on water sustained.

My eyes returned to the solid maelstrom, etched into the smoothness of a wide basin, collecting the effluent of a multitude of minor streams and pulling their waters into the spiralling stasis around the vortex.

Thin lines of red and orange, flowing uncertainly in the dim light of the sun and moon, joined with crystalline trickles of green to pour into the focus of the lenticular pool. Glazed white and pink furrows spun and twisted themselves to form shining helices within the whirlpool's eyes. Liquid blues glittered like colored bottleglass in the various lights, or shone a softer turquoise from within a setting of black ice. And the yellows spun and dazzled...mixing with limes or outlining purples...then whirling onwards and inwards... *moving* at last....

But only in illusion.

I rubbed my eyes and cleared the sweat from my eyebrows and temples, tired of following the colored streamers round and round. I sat down beside Xavier, who was breathing very heavily, his eyes closed, apparently having given up all hope of reaching another side of the plain and all inclination to go on trying.

"It's not that bad," I told him.

"No," he said, struggling for strength. "It's only this illness. It's making things seem far worse than they are. I'm struggling to go on, and struggling to understand. But it's all right. All things pass. There will be another day, I know it. It's just so hard to *feel* it.

"Has time really stopped moving?" I wanted to know, as I glanced up at the frozen sun.

"A gap, perhaps," offered Joaz. "But more likely a fault in ourselves. There's something wrong. But I'll find it. Believe me, I'll find it. We won't be stopped here forever."

"But is there any point in continuing to walk?" I demanded. "Xavier can't go on."

"We must go on," said John definitely. "We can't stop. Even though we seem to be getting absolutely nowhere, accomplishing nothing, we must go on. The drug depends so much on the state of our own minds. As Joaz says, the fault—if fault there is—is within us. We must have courage. And faith."

"Perhaps," I suggested, feeling a sour taste in my mouth, "the fault is only in one of us."

He shook his head.

"We are one, Matthew, for our purposes. One and one only. It's in all of us. We are all within one another."

I bowed my head to avoid his steady gaze. He knew that I didn't know what he was talking about. To him, it didn't matter. Perhaps he was, in his way, *all* of us. I wished that I had a little bit of him in me, to help me and to guide me.

Joaz now was staring at the place which I had abandoned. He seemed transfixed, as no doubt I had been.

At the center of the wheel of color was a deep depression of chitinous black, glistening like polished ebony in the dull light. About this pivot, the pool was arranged in its confusing asymmetry. Although I could no longer see the formation directly, images kept coming back into my mind, brightening and fading with the beating of my heart. It was like a prayer wheel whose praises were color, I thought. It was like a mirror which reflected the whole world. I tried to clear my head by an effort of will. The pictures clung desperately, but were finally dispelled.

"It seems," I said, "that *looking* at things takes far more out of me than it should. As if to stare was to participate actively."

John smiled upon me, as though I had said something of great import. "It is, Matthew," he said. "It is."

"Will the sun never move again?" whispered Xavier.

I touched two fingers to his forehead. He was very hot. Far too hot.

"We must go," pronounced John.

"No!" I protested. "You can't. You'll kill him."

"It will kill us if we stay here."

"A matter of hours. It can't hurt."

"No! It *can* hurt and it *will*. We must go on. It's our *minds* that are important, not our bodies. Courage, faith, hope. That's what matters. *We must go on.*"

And somehow, though I don't remember deciding, we were walking again—not across the great river, nor even in any direction related to that in which we had been travelling, but just walking.

We passed close to the great pool.

All around the uncut jewel, save for the lonely, thin track that we now followed, radiated the threads that fed it, which had given birth to it, which once had sustained its vitality. From all points on the Earth's surface, these torrents made their own mysterious pilgrimage to give their separate gifts of health and brilliance. The essence of the waters of the Earth was gathered here in this timeless instant to give what they had gained, to build itself a deity, a water god, formed in a lost valley, eternal in a moment without time.

And over the new world presided the softly outlined twin lamps and a dancing transience. By their union was the glory seen, by their presence was it lighted. We were strangers here. We had nothing to do with this world. It hardly even existed for us.

"It's not ours, Joaz," said Xavier. "We have no right here."

"We have to go on," said the Brother, doggedly. Joaz, too, I could see all of a sudden, was very. very tired.

"Joaz. do you really believe that we can ever escape?" asked Xavier, in resignation.

John, the leader, turned round without pausing in his stride, and said, "We must have faith."

And faith it was, perhaps, that took us out of that land and on into other ages. I cannot tell.

XVIII.

THE CITY OF ALWAYS NIGHT

We met Raon the Outcast in a city where, he said, it was always night. It was an ancient city, but by now we were in the most ancient of worlds, and there was *nothing* that was not stained by the caresses of thousands of years. Not only that which had been built by Man, but also that which had been born of nature.

While living in an ever-moving present, I had envisaged time as the greatest of all causes. The flow of time, I had thought, determined change, conferred age and development upon all things. Now, I was more inclined to see time as the ultimate in all effects—an arbitrary classification enforced upon the ceaseless random flux of events by the paucity of human understanding, and the lack of perspective.

There was more to the oldness of the city where night was eternal than the mere ticking of a clock.

Raon told us the story of the city. He spoke in the first person, but he also spoke as though he was relating a myth—something not even real, let alone part of his own past.

"I saw her ride down the slope each morning," he told us, "while the brightest of the stars could still be seen in the west, and only the hilltops were lighted by the sun. She rode a horse that was pure white in color. She sat upon a saddle of polished golden leather, and her own robes were yellow and lustrous.

"I followed her as I rode in the sky, with my wings cupped to gather support from the air in order to maintain my glide at her own pace. I would follow her every day, from the moment she appeared to the moment when she left the valley altogether, way beyond this city.

"Once or twice, she would look up and smile at my solitary vigil, and beckon with her eyes. Then, I would float down on the breeze, and hover beside her horse, talking to her about the city, about the valley, and about my love for her. And all the while, the sun would sit peeping out from the eastern horizon, pausing as we crossed the world.

"She never spoke, but only smiled at me. Her lips were smooth and soft. Her face was pale, all except for her eyes, which were deep blue. Every one of her smiles would hurry the words from me, spilling them from my tongue so quickly that I hardly knew what I was saying.

"I told her about my life—about Raon the Outcast who flew in the silent sky of the valley—above the homes of men and below and haunts of the eagles, because both were my enemies. I told her what I thought about, and how it feels when I drift through the heavy air before a storm, or spiral beneath luminous clouds on moonlit nights. I told her that I was neither bird nor man, but something different. But not new, because my kind were on Earth in the earliest days of mankind and birdkind.

"And she would smile, as though she understood.

"So I told her that I loved her, that she was the most beautiful woman in the world, that she was a goddess. My goddess of the dawn, I called her, for that was the moment when she rode over the hill.

"Sometimes, during the late day, when I hid from fearful humankind and the great mountain eagles, I would wonder if she too were an outcast, because of her beauty. Why else would she ride only when the sun was topping the hill?

"Then, the soldiers came, and I was forced to be forever watchful, to find new hiding places and to conceal myself most cleverly when I slept. I lived much closer to the eagles, then, for they were less to be feared. The soldiers tramped the length and breadth of the valley, the sun shining from their armor and the hatred pouring from their eyes. They ate and drank the city's wealth, and left watchers while they slept.

"Inevitably, they discovered my goddess on her lonely rides in the earliest mornings. I tried to warn her, in the stolen moments when I flew beside her.

"No words of love, but words of warning. But to all my words alike, she returned nothing but her gentle smile.

"One day, they lay in wait for her, quietly squatting in the bushes beside the road, just outside the city. I had known that they would. Their eyes were fixed on the top of the hill, or else seeking assurance from each other. They never saw me up in the sky, where I soared—heedless for once of their eyes and their arrows—frantically awaiting the fatal moment when her golden dress, lighted by the half-invisible sun, would appear at the brow of the hill.

"At last she came, and I swooped close to her, darting before her white mount, trying to turn her back. I shouted to her in anguish, begging her to turn away.

"But she smiled her wonderful smile, and rode forward. I dived and fought for height to dive again, struggling to make her understand, to tell her in the language of my desperation that there was danger, that she must not go on.

"And she rewarded my efforts with a host of smiles.

"When she reached the spot where the soldiers hid, they leapt out and took her from the horse. I attacked them, my hands ripping and tearing on the sharp edges of their armor and on the blades of their swords. I wept as my wings were torn by their blows, but frenzy carried me again and again into futile battle. But I wept even more at what I was forced to see.

"I struggled over to where she lay, where they had abandoned us both to our pain and our horror. Her eyes were closed and her golden robe was stained with blood where it had been ripped. I realized, as I watched her face, that when she had come over the hill, the first sunbeams had edged their way into the sky, yet now it was as dark as midnight.

"She opened her eyes, and smiled.

"I realized that the sun would never rise again."

It was a story, and only a story, which Raon told to us in the starlit darkness of the dead city. But time, we knew, often made a mockery of what was real, and made a liar of the truth.

I was beginning, I think, to draw closer to my companions. I no longer needed to ask so many questions. I had learned not to seek reasons, because reasons were only the illusions of our old ways of thinking. Answers there were and would be, but questions no longer needed to be asked.

There was a sickness in Xavier that was sapping his strength little by little.

"We are all ill," Joaz told him. "It is nothing. The remnant of some disease we carried with us from our own world, perhaps. Possibly an effect of the drug."

Raon had left us, once his story was finished, to cry a little to himself for long gone things which never happened. We were left alone in the city of eternal night, deserted by both men and eagles when the sun had refused to shine.

"My stomach is burning," said Xavier. "Bubbles are rising from deep within me, and expanding in my belly to hurt me. I am dying."

I left the two Brothers, and went to John, who was standing some way off looking outward into the starless night.

"He might never see the end of this night," I said, hoping that I was wrong.

"We are forever becalmed," he said, showing the first hint of impatience that I had seen in him for a long while. "Everlasting days and everlasting nights. Where can our destination be?"

"You have the answers," I replied, a little harshly. "*You* have faith. You know that we can and must succeed. Are you beginning to doubt now? Regret, perhaps?"

He turned to look at me, his bright eyes somehow finding light to reflect, deep though they were set in his face. He seemed to draw strength from my every word, whether I encouraged him or taunted him.

"Are you very ill?" he asked. Unsaid, but also in his manner, were the words *we all have doubts. And faith.*

"I have pains. They are not too bad. No fever. But the travelling tells."

He nodded. "That's right," he said. "We are all the same, except that Xavier suffers most. It might well be the drug."

126

"You've never complained," I said. "Nor has Joaz."

"It is for Xavier to complain," he replied. "He has always been a bearer of other men's burdens. A kind man is cruel to himself, Matthew."

"I wouldn't know," I said.

"And yet you seem to suffer more than I."

"I don't understand you."

He shrugged. "We are all one, Matthew. I'm scared, too," he admitted, "but it makes no difference. On we go, until we find what it is that we seek."

"Not Xavier," I said. "Can't we leave him behind?"

"You know we can't."

He turned away, and I replaced him, staring into the infinite darkness. No dawn, the winged man had said. No more dawns. I did not doubt it, though I once would have rejected the idea out of hand rather than fail to understand it.

"Help me," Xavier was pleading, "Help me."

The words struck at my conscience. At the monastery, people had laughed at Xavier. He was always sad, but never made others sad. He had mocked his own sadness, too. But he really had felt things more deeply than the rest of us. Perhaps he did bear a burden for all of us—a burden that would be oursonce again if he were to die.

His cries for help were real enough.

I went back, and knelt beside him. John was also beside him, and Joaz was kneeling, pillowing his friend's head in his hands.

"What can we do, Brother?" I asked.

"It hurts," he complained. "It really hurts. *Really.*" He seemed desperate to convince us, as though he thought that we would not believe in his agony.

"Sleep, Brother," said John, strangely.

"Yes," added Joaz, "sleep for a while, now that it is dark." They had always refused this before.

"Be quiet," said Xavier suddenly. He gripped my arm.

"What is it?" asked Joaz, almost tenderly.

"I can hear someone coming."

There was a distant, haunting sound like a flute being softly blown, without tune, without change of pitch. The note swelled and died irregularly.

"It's a bird," said Joaz. "A night bird."

"The dawn is coming," said John quietly.

"Another day!" Joaz rejoiced. "Xavier...." He looked down, but Xavier was not listening.

"He's dying," said John. "Little by little."

So this was what he had meant by invoking sleep.

He was right. As the sun rose, we watched him fade away into complete stillness.

It was Joaz, Xavier's friend, who stood first, after laying the dead man's head gently upon the ground.

The city had been totally obliterated by the flow of time.

"The outcast spoke the truth," I said. "For the city, at least, it was always night."

XIX.

BENEATH WINTER STARS

In the twilight, it was gray. The crumbling stone, the slit windows, the ivy which shrouded it—all gray. By daylight, it might have seemed serene, a tired building showing its great age in the dust which the wind had eroded from its walls and the stones which the storms had tumbled from the battlements to the mud-caked moat.

But when the shadows of evening and the pale brightness of moonlight descended upon it, a wildness came into the no-longer-sheer walls and no-longer-stern keeps, and made them draw themselves up to a full, fierce height in an echo of former glories. The wrinkles which age had graven were hidden by slashing black shadows which returned the walls to their ancient austerity.

The citadel, by day, was a corpse, a delicate shell, half-forgotten and lost. But when we—only three now—came upon it, at night, it was cloaked in shadow and disguise, waiting through the dark hours with pride.

We came from night to night, for there seemed to be ephemeral daylight only since Xavier had died. We came to invade the citadel, to penetrate it and expose its emptiness, prove its hollowness and deny its pretence.

The big door hung limply from its hinges, and the missing drawbridge had been replaced long ago by stones piled in the waterless moat for form a causeway. By night, the darkness swathed this area, and skillfully hid its dereliction. But on this night, we were here, to step inside the cloak of invisibility, cross the bridge of stones and squeeze between the hanging door and the cool stone wall.

In his right hand, Joaz held a torch to light our way, in his left, a long branch to test the way before us. The atmosphere was full of dust which shone in the flickering torchlight. We stopped to feel the air. I had expected a sensation of infinite weariness and dying majesty, but it was not like that at all. Instead, I found a feeling of strangeness and pungency, and long-distant memory.

We moved through the corridors easily, having no trouble finding our way. But the light we carried was never quite adequate to illuminate the ceiling as well as the floor, and I felt as though we were of no more consequence to the castle than ants of spiders scurrying about its depths.

We came to the great hall—a vast space whose ceiling must have been the roof of the citadel. Its walls were pitted by balconies and windows, which hinted at a multitude of rooms and coverts, stacked like a honeycomb about this central hall. There were seven faces to the hall. The number seven presumably was of some mystic significance to the architects of the castle, for it was an unnatural configuration.

Once there had been oaken tables, chairs and benches in the hall but men long since dead had removed them, leaving small pale scars in the dust where the depth was not quite as great. All that remained was the altar. It had been an altar to a goddess whose half-forgotten form was preserved somewhat inconsistently by images carved at many different times by many different hands upon the vertically-set wooden plaques that surrounded and supported the consecrated stone. Her form was fearsome, her expression wrathful, but her name had been too familiar, or too terrible, to be carved with her aspect, and had been lost. But I knew that her name had not been a pleasant one to the ear, and I knew too that what form she might have had beyond the crude pictures was not pleasant either. She was a goddess of men, but herself inhuman. Men are inclined either to worship that which they hold dear within themselves, or that which is completely unknown and alien.

Joaz paused before the altar, to move his spotlight over it and across the half-obliterated carvings. In shape, the holy stone was simply a raised pedestal, seven-sided and convex on the upper surface. On each of the seven sides was a scene depicting some aspect of the goddess or her worship, but these stone images had suffered more than the wooden ones, and their meaning had become unreadable.

Joaz tapped at them with his pointed stick, trying to clear away some of the clogging dust. But the outer surface of the stone was fragile, and crumbled away under his probing to consign yet more of the images to oblivion.

He held the torch upwards, then, and scanned the carvings in the wood, committing each of his memory as though to be sure that he would recognize the goddess should he ever see her. Joaz had been a silent man since Xavier had died, and I feared that he too might follow. He seemed to have accepted Xavier's share of our collective burden on to his shoulders alone, and the illness was evident in the way he walked, and in the way his face was lined with strain.

We passed through the cloister-like arches which supported the lowest of the many balconies around the hall, and into the haphazard maze of rooms piled up irregularly like a tumbled heap of blocks, without symmetry or apparent logic. We wound our way among them, weaving and meandering, around the circumference of the castle.

John showed none of his usual impatience. He seemed to have accepted that we could not force a pace upon the flow of time, rather the other way about.

Sometimes we discovered the gray outer wall, in which time had pecked tiny holes where moonlight filtered through. More often we came out above the high wall, looking out into apparently limitless darkness. The steady tapping of Joaz's stick assured us that the way we chose was solid and safe. As we circled, we spiralled upward, a slight gradient here, a brief fragment of staircase there. The walls were almost bare, devoid of fungus or vermin, but rich with choking dust, left in the wake of time. Our footsteps echoed faintly as they stirred the carpet of silence and reached the cold stone beneath. But the echoes were faded, muffled by the peace of antiquity. Sometimes they would sound like the chanting of distant voices, and I laughed once or twice at that. But my laughter produced sharper echoes, like the throb of dancing feet and measured voices raised in staccato prayer, and I would have to stop while my heart calmed down again.

Occasionally, as we passed a balcony or alcove that gave on to the central hall, the corner of my eye would catch the glimmer of an image, and record the impression of fire-light sending supple shadows scrambling up the wall. But when I turned and my eyes looked full upon the opening, the deception would be plain. And when, once, I stepped forward to stare into the ill-lit gloom, there would be nothing at all, save the invisible, brooding altar and the dust.

As we ascended the paths of the citadel, the impression became more pronounced. The chanting that rose and fell under cover of our echoes was more precise, and might have been an unknown, fluid language. Once, when John stopped us to listen, the eerie chant continued. I knew then that we all felt the same thing, and that it was no illusion of mine alone. The first hint of weakness forced us to continue, drowning the purring voices with our footsteps and the unsteady scraping of Joaz's stick.

The shadows, too, high on the walls of the heptagonal column, took a shape, like whirling figures, twisting to the tune of the chant, with long hair streaming from their heads and supple arms moving like waves upon the sea.

But when we halted to peer more closely, when we strained our ears to catch the half-audible rhythm, there was silence and darkness. And so we went on, up and up, around and around, till our minds reverberated with half-heard sounds and half-seen sights. Even I had found the courage to force back my fear, but the others would not have turned back in any case. I had no choice but to follow. Not until our examination was complete would John allow himself to be turned aside, to walk casually back along empty passageways and out into the night again.

But the flickering persisted. No flame of ours cast those momentary shadows, nor echo of our movement formed the rhythmic chant. They were echoes of another sort—the reflection of the past, a residue hiding the face of time.

In themselves, they offered no harm, were neither frightening nor aggressive. It was their transience and the fact that

I could not detect their origin that disturbed me, because they made me doubt myself.

We passed a window to the exterior—a pitiful vertical slash built for defense rather than to allow the ingress of light. It was silent outside—the quiet slumber of ordinary night—with only the gleam of winter stars and the glare of the mad moon disturbing its easiness. It was the same landscape we had left, a fact which soothed me for some reason which I could not analyze.

It was here, at the furthest part from the seven-sided grand hall, that I heard the musical voices undulating in my ears, and knew with a certainty that they were fully arrived at last, and would persist. There was no immediate outlet to the hall for the fire-shadows to show themselves, and we began to wind our way back to look for them.

The balcony to which we came was the topmost one. Roofed by the giant beams and badly mortared slabs of rock and slate of the very ceiling of the castle, it looked out directly opposite the ornate altar, hundreds of feet below. Their rhythm was clear now, and so were those which sang the words, and those which cast the shadows, far below us. Joaz lowered his torch and doused it in the dust. It was no longer needed.

In front of the altar was a gigantic fire, which hurled its flames high into the air, and whose smoke misted the room and imparted a touch of surrealism that my own imagination was incapable of supplying.

Around the fire and the altar was a semicircle of squatting figures, small, almost dwarfed, shining with firelight reflected from their sweat-polished bodies. They swayed to the chant which issued from their mouths. Tiny, shaven skulls with sunken, pin-bright eyes surmounted stunted, naked bodies which swung liquidly from side to side in perfect harmony and pendular consistency.

Outside the semicircle was a haphazard grouping of worshippers—the rich and poor squatting in random pattern on their night of equality, before their deity.

Men and women clothed in velvet, lace, leather, and cowhide sat as though mesmerized before the lunatic flames and the maddening grace of the swaying priests. They were still, not moving with the monotonous pulse of the prayer, although it must have seized their minds and twisted them into a chaos of fanaticism in which the world was gone and the goddess was all. The aristocratic and the miserable, the envious and the graceful, the hated and the radiant—all wore identical expressions, all were thinking identically, for this was the moment of identity. This was the time when that which makes a blind cripple the same as a princess was forced to the forefront of their consciousness.

Within the boundary marked by the line of priests, within the area commanded by the great goddess, danced figures whose shadows gyrated upon the wall. There were three—all women—and they were erect, moving easily, and with a beauty that was only part their own. They belonged to the goddess, they *were* the goddess, for they were within the semicircle of the priests. And for this reason their faces did not bear the uniform expression of clotted devotion which the worshippers wore, nor were they animated corpses like the blindly chanting puppet priests. These dancers were alive, wholly and absolutely, with a life that was alien and unnatural, because each of them was more than the whole glut of mere humanity without. Their faces were the multiple faces of the goddess, supernal, suffused with an unholy beauty and splendor. The wrath of the sculpted pictures was not even hinted at—perhaps it referred to a different aspect, perhaps it was symbolical, perhaps it was paramount only in the imagination of the various artists. Whatever the reason, it was not here, in the *reality*. It was not that the goddess was benign—there was power and grandeur in the reflected stature of the dancers, but the emotions were not the emotions of men.

Suddenly, with terrifying grace and smoothness, one of the dancers spun into the flames. The satin of her clothes and her long silken hair blossomed immediately into flame, and then her body began to burn. Yet, the dance continued—not the spasmodic, sickening dance of the dead, but the fluid expression of life.

Not until the whirling figure was almost consumed did she fall to clutch the fire more intimately, and only then, it seemed, did she die. Her death made impression neither on the other dancers, the singing priests, nor the glass-eyes worshippers.

And, in their turn, each of the remaining dancers pirouetted within the flames, maintaining life for infinite moments, then falling soundlessly—scorched skeletons.

Then came the goddess. Embodied in the substance of their sacrifice, the odor of charcoal and the miasma of their moment of passing, She rose from the flames. Hers was no mere coalescing of smoke, nor image within the soul-twisting flames. Hers was a presence as real as the seven walls of the hall, as real as the people who worshipped Her. From the three reflections of Her beauty, She had come at the moment of their unity within the fire.

She twisted slowly in a grotesque mime of the dance of Her surrogates, entwining Herself amongst the flames and swirls of smoke. She was huge. Although encapsulated within the aura of the flames, She filled the grand hall with Her magnificence and power. She was handsome. In Her image no woman had even been shaped—the race of Man was merely more of the substance on which Her foot rested, the clay beneath Her feet. She was alive, with a wonderful, vibrating life which filled Her worshippers and turned their outward-yearning thoughts within themselves to search.

And for a moment, as She turned, star-hair drifting behind Her, Her pale marble eyes met those of Joaz as he craned forward from the high balcony, obscuring both my view and John's for an instant. Perhaps there followed a softening of the tempered power in Her handsome face, perhaps a fleeting expression of some alien emotion. In that instant, Joaz's eyes took on a diamond stare, and the lines of his face were the lines of a hundred faces far below him. His consciousness, almost his sentience, seemed to be slipping away from his hawk-like face, and he was one of them—one of the worshippers, the pagans, the idolaters....

Then it was daylight, and he was whole again. Around us was a swamp of silver-scummed water patched with islands of warped pines and dead brown grass. A dewy winter sun shone in the south east.

"Matthew," said Joaz urgently, in a hoarse whisper. John behind him, was cradling his head drunkenly between his hands.

"Yes."

"We're adrift," he said. "Adrift in chaos. It isn't the future. It *isn't*. There isn't any future any more. Time has stopped dead, and perception is breaking down. *Find the Afterman*, Matthew. Find *him*, and there will be order again made from chaos. But you must find him."

"We will, Joaz," I promised. "We will."

Before he died, he looked once more at John.

"Look after him, Matthew," he said.

"I will," I promised, again.

XX.

SINGER OF DREAMS

"There is music in my soul and poetry in my heart...."
The lantern-like sun hung heavily in the lilac-colored sky, slowly falling into the west. The music floated on the tired, humid air, and I climbed the hill with sweat on my face. John was just behind me.
"But music is a parody and poetry false reflection...."
I heard the notes as though from a great distance, although the singer was not very far away. The emotion they stirred in my mind was unfamiliar, yet I somehow identified it with nostalgia.
"No man who knows them takes full pride in his art...."
Certainly no memories of mine could give nostalgia to those weird notes. Their beauty and strangeness were unlike any music I had ever heard drawn from a harp before.
"For in no way may he honestly author his affection...."
I could see him now—a tiny, hunched figure in a long white garment which draped about his shoulders and cast shadows over his harp. His head was bent, and I saw him shake it ponderously as his ancient hand dropped from the still-quivering strings. It was hard to imagine that his voice could have sounded those haunted words, or that his wrinkled hands could ever have caressed the strings so cleverly. Yet the harp had played, his lips had moved.
He saw me. His eyes were sunken, almost invisible within his skull, and shadowed by sprawling eyebrows. His cracked lips moved to parody a smile as I drew close, with John trailing in my wake.

"You are looking for me?"

"No, not in particular," I replied.

The old man nodded, and his head stayed bowed. "I am the singer of dreams," he said, his voice slow and muffled.

"My name is Matthew. My brother John is beside me."

"Why have you come?" he asked. His voice was harsh, leaving no resemblance to that of the singer I had heard while coming up the hill. And yet he was the same.

"We have come a great distance," I said, "in search of a being whose shape we do not know."

"How, then, will you recognize him when you find him?"

"I don't know," I confessed.

"When we find him," said John, "we will know." He spoke with the confidence of his faith, but I was not so sure.

"People came to see me," said the old man. "To see a strange man who has lived for many generations, who has seen too much, and who sings with voices not his own. To stare, or to listen, they came."

I made no answer.

"There are always stories," said the dream singer. "Do you believe them?"

"What stories?" I asked.

"I am an old man," he continued, ignoring my question, "and I dream. With my harp, I sit and I see. Where the dreams come from, I do not know. How can I know? I see them as though they were my own, but they do not belong to me. Out of the past and out of the distance they come. They are not mine—they only echo in my mind. I cannot tell you why.

"So many things I have seen. Many I could not comprehend, and many more I would not. I have lived through many centuries, and have dreamed but cannot understand.

"Once, that sun...." He raised a hand to point at the crimson sun. "I remember when the sun...."

He dropped his hand, and the sentence remained incomplete. I was a little afraid. I too remembered the sun in the days when it had been blinding yellow instead of dull red.

"What do you dream?" asked John quietly.

"I will sing you a dream," he said. "Which dream? Tell me, what is the thing you most fear in all the world?"

"Loneliness," I said, the answer coming so readily to my lips that even I could not be sure that it was true.

"Very well," he said softly. "I will sing you a dream of loneliness. Whose dream, I cannot tell."

His gnarled fingers brushed the harp strings. He opened his mouth and sang. This was not the voice he had used before, nor was it his own voice. This was a new voice, a plaintive one with a strong breath of hopelessness.

There were no words to the song, and yet the music captured my mind and made pictures arise within me. I could not tell whether it was the harp or the voice which entranced me. Perhaps the combination of both.

There were storm clouds frowning upon a dull sea, whereupon a single ship floated. She had but one mast, and that carrying little sail, yet she ran fast before the wind, creaking with the effort. Three birds—petrels—bounced past, skittering madly over the slow, gross waves. In the distance was a row of cliffs, jagged and toothed, but high and forbidding. The ship ran for them, and I felt an ambiguity in the situation—that land could mean either safety or destruction.

The lone man aboard the ship did not know whether to hope or despair because the ship rushed headlong for the strange coast. The clouds seethed and boiled up above, and shed torrential rain upon the wings of the wind.

He whispered a name once, twice, as the ship gathered more and more speed. He did not pray. His voice was not afraid. Just a name, suggestive of long-lost love and time-depleted dreams. Lightning smashed, and thunder drowned the name so that I could not hear what it was. The face of the cliffs loomed close and terrible, and the sea split into foam ahead of the ship's course, to show jagged black teeth reaching from the sea to tear the ship apart. She flashed straight into the black smile of the reef, exploding with the shock of the first impact.

The man was gone, and the name he had spoken consigned forever to the depths of the sea.

The sound died, the strings quivered and were still. The dream singer seemed frozen, arched over the harp.

"What happened?" I asked.

The dream singer did not look up. "He died. But I think he was a good man. What name did he give to the storm, I wonder? That is all I know. I see the sky and the sea, and the crooked cliff. But I cannot see what lies *behind*. I cannot read his thoughts. I do not know his feeling. I do not even know the name which he whispered, lost as it was in the sound of the sea."

"You were not this man?" I said.

"Yes," he replied. "I was the man. I was a million men and women. I live a thousand moments that I do not own. All of them are me, but I am not one of them. I am the singer of dreams. That is all."

His fingers brushed the strings again, almost unwillingly, and again the voice—*another* voice—took me away into somewhere else, to share another dream.

A winged girl lay on a low-sweeping bough of a great willow which stood beside a pool, her pale blue wings dropping listlessly as she stirred the surface of the water with her tiny feet. Her eyes stared up through the gently swaying foliage to the crystalline sky.

A necklace of golden flowers clung to her shoulders, and trailing, flowerbearing vines formed loose garments, enfolding her like a chiton. A cloying odor of nectar surrounded her.

Her eyes slowly turned downward from her contemplation of the sky, and she rolled off the bough. Then, before her fall could break the surface of the pool there was a great clapping like a frenzied drumbeat, and she was away into the air, only her toes touching the water.

She danced and pirouetted high above the branches of the willow. She ascended until she seemed to be a tiny speck in a sea of deeper blue. Higher, and yet higher, until she disappeared. The willow's branches seemed to move, although there was no wind, and then they quivered and beat the air, groping at seven rose-colored petals which floated down from the sky.

And then she fell. Pain was marked with appalling clarity upon her face. Her breasts heaved as she fought for air. Her miniature hands clutched at emptiness and her legs thrashed. But still she fell as though she was caught in a sucking vortex. Not until the last possible moment, when it was all but inevitable that her body would smash into the earth, did the wingbeat begin to have effect. Her fall slowed and, sobbing, she caught the branches of the willow and hung by slender arms, her hair cascading over her eyes, her garlands ripped and loose.

She lay on a low-sweeping bough of the willow, her pale blue wings quivering slightly as they drooped, feeble and futile. Her tears disturbed the surface of the pool, running down her cheeks as she stared up through the loving foliage to the crystalline sky.

"She was a dryad, you see," explained the dream singer, when the image had faded away. "She was bound to the tree. She couldn't leave it. So her wings weren't any use to her. Not really."

"You have beautiful dreams," I said to him.

"Not I," he replied. "It is *you* who have beautiful dreams. Your brother and yourself. All of you. They're all your dreams."

"You have none of your own?" I asked.

"Only one."

"Tell me."

"That one is mine. Yet the harp must play. Listen to me."

The new notes buffeted my ears and filled my eyes with tears. He sang in a new voice—a voice that was at once so new and so familiar that I raised my hand to my lips lest it should be myself that sang and not he. I was stilled as the music took hold of me, focused on me, whirled around me. I wondered for a dying moment whether I also was a part of the singer of dreams, an actor in one of his stories. Then, there was only the music...

I was in a garden, where there were golden fountains surmounted by plumes of vapor and fine sprays of water. I had come to find something I had forgotten in growing older. And I had come to seek something new as well—something that only existed in this garden, in this moment of time. I had come to search for something I had left behind long ago. A face, a memory, a person. I had come to bury my regrets, to look upon a love that might have been mine, and to wonder why I had lost it, so long before. I knew why. Ambition, or some such thing, had taken me in treacherous arms and led me far and wide to chase a will-o'-the-wisp—an idle dream whose shape I had not even known.

I had not come to ask for forgiveness, but for hope. Which, I knew, was by far the greater thing, for to return into memory is impossible, whereas to know that there is something yet to come is faith. I was asking for a reason for the beating of my heart, for continuing to grope in the dark, looking for the light of day.

It is said that hope beats eternally within the human breast, but I knew that was not so. For I had no hope—my heart was a captive of remorse, and had no dreams to free it. I had sought fulfillment, but I had come to know that it was to be found only here, in the garden.

I asked for the mists to be cleft by sight and sound. I asked to be carried from my captivity. I asked for a memory to open her lips, to let me hear tears in her eyes. I asked for hope.

I heard nothing but the callous hiss of the fountain. But then, something new, something strange. The tides of time were turning. The air had wings of song..."

"Matthew," I heard John's voice saying, "It's only a dream. It's over."

Again, the village near the three peaks.

Again, the magical sound of the harp.

I faced the singer of dreams, whose eyes were hidden by his massive white brows.

"Was that your dream or mine?" I asked.

"It was mine, as I said," he replied. "But perhaps yours too. Why may we not find ourselves in the dreams of others?"

The last threads of the dream died, tremulously from my mind. The strings were sighing in the wind, but I knew they had been stilled for some time.

"How did it end?" I asked him. "*Where* did it end?" I was not sure what I had seen, at the end of the dream, whether or not it was an artifact of my own imagination.

The dream singer looked up, and I saw his eyes. They were a deep violet, the color of the evening sky. They were dampened with tears and the pupils were mere pinpricks. I stood still, not attempting to recover from the state of profound emotional shock in which the dream had left me. I think that I was close to death in that moment.

"She was dead," stated the dream singer, simply.

No reward. No redemption. No hope. No turning back. One way only. EXIT on the *other* side of the door.

"She was dead."

The second time, the words reached me, and I swayed giddily. My thoughts were muddled, mingled with strange new emotions and implications.

John caught me, and held me.

"Didn't you see it?" I said to him.

"I was there."

"It was my dream."

"Yes, I know. I remember."

"It was my dream."

"It was his too," said John. "You're not alone. There's nothing new."

"I don't believe it."

"No," he said. "I don't suppose you do."

The dream singer sat, still as marble, for a minute more. Then his aged body seemed simply to collapse. His lips quivered, the snow-strands in his beard vibrating like harp strings. His back heaved, as long, racking sobs threatened to shake his aged frame apart.

"She was dead," I repeated slowly, and I began to understand.

XXI.

THE SEA OF BLOOD

The tower stood alone in the ocean, like a needle set in the slumbering surface of a sea the color of sultry wine. The water was dyed a deep red in reflecting the image of a ruddy sky.

The clouds, great splashes of maroon, drifted idly back and forth across the sky, merging and then tearing apart, trailing rubicund beads of aerial perspiration in the humid atmosphere. The sky, or as much of it as was visible, was striped and barred, blotched and smudged with a mixture of gentle pinks, flushed reds and handsome magentas. On the horizon, dust hung like rich drapes, reflecting red lights like the sea and the clouds.

The sea was like a mirror of darkly-glowing, cherry-red molten glass, calm and still as a stagnant pond. No wind stirred its serenity, nothing was visible beneath the unruffled plane of its surface. No weeds floated, no bright fish darted around the cylindrical base of the tower.

Red—everything was red; the sky, the clouds, the dust. Even the lustrous surface of the steel tower shone red, for there was no other color to reflect. It was as though we were floating in a liquid trapped in the loculus of a red crystal ball. The whole world seemed a living wound, flooded with arterial blood.

Far above, while we watched incredulously, the lazy clouds bestirred themselves and jostled in a hurried mass flow, as though a sudden wind had picked them up and immediately abandoned them again. From their edges, vapor spun away to dissipate like smoke, but their bulk seemed unaltered.

And then the surface of the ocean was disturbed. A ripple spread slowly outward. And another, another...and the sea came to violent life as the sky rained blood where we were standing, the raindrops blurred the scene and turned it into a patternless miasma. At this close range, we could see through the raindrops. They were water, not blood.

I turned away to look at John by my side. Behind us, not having joined us in our wandering stare, was the singer of dreams.

"Is this real?" I asked to no one in particular, and then to the dream singer. "Or is it another of your illusions?"

"All my illusions are real," stated the white-haired man.

"But are we here, or will we wake in a few moments to find ourselves back on that same hillside?"

"The hillside has gone," said the singer of dreams. "We are here, in this place."

"Then you can move through time as well?"

"There is no time any more," John reminded me.

"I don't know," I confessed. "Sometimes one thing seems to be time, sometimes another. If there is no time, what changes? If there is time, why can we not see the change?"

"It's chaos, Matthew," replied John. "Time was only the *order* of events. A human imposition. We've always had to make the world artificial in order to cope with it, because our minds are inadequate to accept the reality. Animals work by instinct—stimulus and reaction. We work by *Time*—the ordering of change to suit our artificial system called logic, or reason, or cause-and-effect. Our perception has changed. We've seen too much. We've seen things that we can't fit into the pattern, and our minds have abandoned it altogether.. It only worked in a very limited way, within a very small field. The other time travelers, they didn't come far enough, they didn't see enough. Whether your life spans seventy years or two hundred and seventy makes little difference. We've seen *all* of it Matthew. From beginning to end. Trillions of years. Because we *came* to see. We came to find answers, not to escape. We've lost time. Forever."

Then how, I wanted to know, were we ever to find what we came to see? If we were adrift in chaos, how were we ever to locate a specific being? Joaz, before he died, had given me an answer—find the Afterman, and he can bring order out of the chaos. At the end of chaos is a new order. The order of an entirely new perception.

But was it true? How could Joaz possibly know?

John didn't know. I could see that. He had his faith, still, but that was all. His dream had proved too great for him. He had striven so hard to *see* and to *understand*, and he'd failed. He would have given up entirely, had it not been for faith.

We came, he had said, to find answers, and not to escape. But had we? He, I felt sure, had tried to escape, and failed. I had been escaping for many years—inwardly, not outwardly—from the dream which the old man and the harp had brought back to me, and its tragic conclusion. Neither of us, I believed, had come only to find answers.

But there were only answers left, now. And dreams. And faith.

"I don't know why the sky is red," the singer of dreams was saying to John. "I don't understand. Yet I created this world. I made it, with my harp."

"Then it's only another dream?" asked John.

"I don't know," confessed the old man. "Sometimes I'm not sure what I create."

John looked at me—a sharp, significant look whose meaning I failed to interpret. To avoid it, I turned to the window and watched the huge drops of water falling from the dark clouds, the spray hazing the surface of the water. Faster and harder it fell, as the sky sought to unburden itself within a few, brief minutes. And slowly, while I watched, it began to ease again.

The sky and the horizon were visible once more—not sharply defined, because red is not an abrupt color, but they were there, no longer hidden in the confusion. Several hundred yards from the tower base a black head burst into the red world. Like a seal's, it was round and sleek. It rose above the waves on a silky snake's neck which seemed to have no end. Up and up it swept, until, at last, a leviathan's streamlined upper body heaved itself half-above the surface, the rest of the massive body hidden beneath the red waves, and the ripples kicked up by its vast flippers expanded all around it.

"Another," said John, who had joined me when I gasped at the creature's appearance. He pointed to a second black head rising out of the sea.

The beasts had faces, which seemed to beam in imbecile fashion, with small pin-point eyes set well forward, and minute ears on the sides of the head. Their whole bearing was seal-like; they had fur, of the smoothed-down slick type characteristic of seals. Only the long neck and the colossal bulk alienated the creature from the seals. Their ancestors? I wondered. Perhaps their descendants? Or simply the coincidence of similar adaptation?

"I wonder what they are?" said the dream singer, pensively. Sometimes he seemed all-wise, at other times like a small child wondering at everything. He seemed to have as many minds as he had voices.

"Your subjects, creator," replied John. Why he should choose to mock the old man, I did not know. Perhaps other things had been said while I was busy with my own thoughts.

The singer of dreams ignored him, and went on with his quiet contemplation of the animals.

John carefully studied the palm of his hand, whether annoyed or ashamed I could not tell.

"Life will always survive in the sea," I said, watching the two beasts moving toward one another through the red water. "Even if there is no Afterman, the line will not end. The human race will become merely a side branch. An unsuccessful attempt. Something else will come out of the sea."

"That must not be," stated John.

"Why not? Your Brotherhood preaches humility and acceptance. The race of Man is not the be-all and end-all of existence. Why should we even lay claim to a place on the main line? Isn't that vanity too?"

"But all that effort wasted. All that potential lost."

"Nothing is wasted, John," I told him, with a hint of triumph at winning the exchange, "because time is an artifact. It doesn't matter to the strategy of life."

He looked at me again, his deep-set eyes both accusing and admitting his mistake. I thought for a moment that I had trespassed on his previous faith, but that was not what occupied his mind.

"You're getting better, Matthew," he said.

"I haven't felt the illness since the citadel of the goddess," I said.

"That's not what I mean."

I hadn't really supposed that it was. Why must the boy always speak in riddles, as though life was a drama with many meanings?

The dream singer was watching the animals moving in wide, slow circles, as though each was chasing the other but not really interested in catching up. They were moving their tiny heads from side to side.

"Do you know what they're doing?" he asked suddenly.

I contemplated the circular path for a moment. "No," I said.

"Making love," he said, and laughed softly into his beard. John sighed.

The clouds had moved aside, revealing the full red eye of the sun. It was still hazy, and the rain still fell gently. Across the sky, to the north, was a rainbow. A red rainbow. A gigantic arch in the sky, it gave a promise to Mankind long-dead. I smiled wryly at the ambassador from the creator of chaos.

"Here we are," said the singer of dreams, happening on a new thought, "adrift in the world's blood. And for all we seem to care, it might be water."

It didn't sound very funny, and I didn't laugh. There was some relationship between the singer of dreams and this world that I couldn't understand. Perhaps he and his harp really had created it. Perhaps there was nothing else left in all the world except for him and his echoed dreams.

XXII.

THE LAKE OF LIGHT

We came to the lake of light—John, the singer of dreams and myself—from the high tower that stood alone in the sea of blood. There was nothing in between, and yet I was taken by the impression that we had come a long way; that we had passed over tall hills and through deep forests, and that the dream singer had carried his harp over many a long mile. I began to wonder whether my memory might not be playing me false.

Certainly, there seemed to be more knowledge of the dream singer in my mind than our short acquaintance could have put there. I could summon pictures of his wandering the world—*our* world, from which we had set out on this mad pilgrimage—with no one challenging his right to pass or questioning his strange appearance. I could see him striding along, with the harp in his arms, yet not burdening him— nay, almost as if the harp was in some way assisting him. Never did he suffer lack of food, nor lack of a bed at night, although never could I see him handling a coin. Sometimes, in these evenings which never happened, he would sing— deep, slow melodies of other travellers in fantastic lands. But always there was a hint of the *known*, the emotion that was so real that it might be my own, the element of the common- place in a grotesque landscape of imagination. So real were these songs to me that I struggled to remember times when I might have heard them.

I contemplated the notion that the memories I had were only the dreams, and that these ghost memories were real ones—that we had never traveled in time at all. But that was not satisfactory. I thought it more likely that part of the dream singer was seeping into me, that his absorption of other men's parts, other men's dreams was so powerful that his own personality and existence was oozing out in some sort of exchange.

Above all, I wondered, could the singer of dreams be the Afterman? But John said nothing and I was afraid to hazard such a guess. One thing that seemed clear was that the dream singer led us now. John, always the leader and the impetus before, was now taking a minor role, allowing the other to choose the way and provide the motive force.

The dream singer seemed to know where he was going, yet he never named a destination to either one of us. I think it possible that he followed the path that he did because it was the way assigned to him, and he had no more idea than we where it might end up.

When we came to the shores of the lake of light, however, I was sure that here was an ending; that something lay in the pearly glitter of the insubstantial sea of color that might provide some clue, some answer. How we were to set sail upon the bowl of light, I did not know, but I knew that at the correct time, as we walked the shore, we would find some way. My only explanation for all these thoughts and strange knowledge was that they were leakage from the singer of dreams or his harp.

We walked the golden beach for several miles, continually turning our eyes to the hazed glow of the lake. Our footprints were deep in the sand, and lonely as they stretched back to where a mist of colored light eclipsed them. As we walked, I felt sure I saw shapes of the eddying pools of quicksilver-like substance. I saw faces expressing emotions, people and non-people acting out strange mimes in the eerie brilliance.

I felt that there was an affinity between the lake of light and the harp, each in their own way a mirror and a memory of the race whose whole existence flowed into the old man as dreams. I wondered whether the lake might not have its own dream singer—a human vector for its well of knowledge and emotion.

Suddenly, we came upon the boat. It was a small row-boat, without oars, and it seemed oddly commonplace and vulgar in this fantasy world beyond the far-reaching grasp of Time. Silently, but with a glitter in his violet, half-hidden eyes, the dream singer seated himself in the bow of the boat and carefully laid the harp between his knees. John and I sat in the other seat, facing the dream singer, not knowing what to do but content to wait and see.

Slowly, without a hint of disturbance in the smoky sea of color, the boat slid out on to the surface of the lake of light. Suddenly, the mist was all around us. I could see neither the shore we had left, nor whatever it might be that we travelled towards. Even the sky was chaotically bejewelled with living streamers of color.

The silence oppressed me. The dream singer never shifted his position, nor said a single word. The harp strings were still, and I found myself wishing that he would play, and bring an old, familiar dream to banish this place from my mind. Almost without volition I reached out and stroked the strings myself—a thing I never would have dared before. The dream singer stared at me with neither surprise nor anger as I felt the strings frozen rigid—I could not stir them.

I turned away to the gently swaying colors which ran past the boat. Again, I was certain that I saw faces in the mist, silent faces that communicated with one another, but never with me.

Then, more to break the heavy silence than because I was convinced, I said, "I think I see a face that I knew."

"I knew them all...once," said the dream singer quietly. As we penetrated more deeply into the miasma of random color, the mist drew in so tightly that the figure of the old man in the bow became increasingly complicated with a drifting dust of light, which at times illuminated him and at others threw him into deepest of shadow, all the while maintaining an ever-changing kaleidoscopic effect which confused and frightened me more than any other of the strange things I associated with the singer of dreams.

"How long must we travel this way?" I was at last driven to inquire.

"No longer than necessary," his voice replied from obscurity. He must have observed the fear in my words, for he added, "Forget that there is a man in the colored shadows. Do not try to see me, because the more you try, the easier it will be to lose me."

I was glad of John's presence beside me, for him I could *feel* as well as see. There was no way to lose his being in the mist, though his outlines, too, were beginning to waver and change as the light began to play weird games with the lines I knew to be solid and real, and those I imagined to be mere illusions.

At times, the dream singer became so hidden that he took on strange pseudoforms, like an ape or a great bird. Once, he was a harp, and I almost heard strings trilling, but the silence prevailed and the illusion was gone within a moment. I wondered what strange shapes the mist made out of my brother and myself for *his* eyes.

Finally, the confusion won. "I cannot see at all now," I said.

"Nor can I," said John. "But shut your eyes, if you want, and rely on other senses. I'm here beside you."

"Are your eyes shut?" I wanted to know.

"Yes."

I shut mine. I could feel the solid wood of the boat beneath my feet and my buttocks. I could feel my clothes making contact with John's all the way down my left side. I could even hear his breathing, I think.

"It's real," I said. "It is real."

"Nothing is real," said the dream singer, "save one thing, and that one thing is more than you or I or the lake of light."

I ignored him.

"The harp is real, isn't it?" said John.

"A part of it. The whole universe is a part of it."

"And what is it?"

"You will see, in time. Our passage is almost over."

Both of them relaxed into silence once again, and I diverted my attention to the light which englobed us, ready to shut my eyes again if I became confused or afraid. My whole world seemed to be a body of glass, erratically flawed and silvered to form miniature mirrors, and transparent to the point at which I could see through it to eternity. At times, the light echoed, resonated and floated as though there was a logic to the whole pattern which somehow evaded me. It seemed that all the properties one might ascribe to matter, space, and time as discrete entities were here united into a whole, basic form.

And, slowly, the mist began to thin again. The dream singer's figure shaded into the same half-formed shapes as before, into tantalizing darkness and illumination, and finally into himself.

The air cleared gradually of its mosaic colors. and faces faded into the far distance and were lost. We were alone.

"There," said the dream singer, and pointed.

It was like a city—curving minarets and pagodas, spires and stark edges, all of a substance like colloidally suspended light, as though the lake had coalesced into a series of three-dimensional paintings.

I understood, for a moment, something of the kinship between the lake and the harp that the dream singer carried. Here was all the *sight* in the world; in the harp was all the *hearing*. Another diversion of dreams, that's all it was.

"You created this, too!" I accused him.

"I'm trying to," he said. "But it's very difficult. I'm trying to catch it all, but there's such a great deal. Someday, though, I'll build far more than that city. I'll build a whole universe. I'll build something of which the whole universe is only a part."

"What is this place?" asked John, who sat looking up at the arrayed towers and domes.

"It is mine." he replied simply.

"But what is it meant to *be*?" he wanted to know. His voice contained an urgency, as though he was on the brink of something important. I didn't have to ask what.

"It is all of me. My knowledge, my memories, my many shapes and my emotions. It is my every thought expressed as a single unit, my every dream fulfilled. It is the limit of my creation."

"The limit?" questioned John bitterly. "Can there be nothing more? You're old, but you need not die."

153

"I have no more time."

"No." A note of resignation in John's voice.

I was silent, my eyes following the curves which went on and on forever.

"You're not the Afterman, are you?" continued John. His voice was very sad now, not accusing. He'd given up blaming the dream singer for what he wasn't. "You're only another step on the way. You're more than we are, but you're still not enough."

"Things don't change just like that, John," I reminded him. "It takes time."

"There is no time. *All* change is here."

"But there are still steps. Still intermediates. The Afterman has to *develop*, John."

"But he's *here* somewhere."

Is he? I wondered.

I looked at the dream singer then, as he wrapped his twisted fingers around his harp and hugged it to him. And I wondered something else. Suppose he *had* been the Afterman. What then?

Yes, indeed. What then?

"I'm sorry," said the singer of dreams, once more sweeping the strings of his harp into life, so that a tune of grandeur and triumph swelled into the shattering silence. "I am only who I am."

XXIII.

THE LAST MAN

The man came up the hill towards us. The dream singer hummed wordlessly to the soft melody of his harp, but his eyes never left the stranger. The man was tall and dark and cadaverous, with short hair and abnormally long arms.

"I know you," he said to the dream singer.

The old man calmed the harp strings. "I am the singer of dreams."

"And *I*," said the stranger pretentiously, "am the last man." He glanced at me, as though daring me to contradict him, and I could not meet his eye. John did, but he said nothing.

"What do you want with me?" asked the dream singer.

"I wish to travel with you a little way. I think that you can take me where I need to go."

"You have a destination?" asked the old man, leaning over the harp. "What does the last man need of a destination? Where is there for you to go?"

The dark man's eyes closed. "You won't take me, then?"

The dream singer laughed quietly. "Of course."

"Of course," echoed the other. "You can't deny me, can you?"

"Why should I do that? I'm an old man. Nine hundred years I've lived and there are uncounted centuries before that living within me, flowing through me. And now you are the last, save for the travelers in time. I'll take you wherever you want to go."

The last man shook his head slowly. "Nine hundred years," he repeated. But he did not say it reverently, as had the singer of dreams, nor with a hint of awe, as I might have said it. His voice was dull, as though the mere mention of time had lost its meaning. And perhaps it had. I wondered whether he might have been impressed had I told him how many years John and I had seen. Probably not.

"Where do you want to go?" asked the singer of dreams.

"Where only the harp can take me."

The old man nodded. Without any further speech, he picked up the harp and set off down the hill. The sea was hidden at this point by a rise in the ground, but I knew that we were within a hundred yards of the shore. John had followed him, as John still seemed content to do, even though he had surrendered the idea that we might have found the Afterman.

The last man walked with me for a few minutes, and then went forward to walk alongside the singer of dreams.

In front of us was the giant eye of the sun, which seemed to shed less light every time we saw it. It burned dark red now. Behind us were the mountains and the forests. We had come to some land with the semblance of the one we had left behind. There was nothing here that we could not have seen in our own time. Chaos was composed of fragments of everywhere, and not everything had been reshaped by creators such as the singer of dreams.

The edge of the sea at this place was a long, straight bank of broken black rock. There was no beach, merely a few small inlets where sand collected. We came on to a ledge of rock. Many feet below us the sullen waves sagged lifelessly against the pitted face of rock. The dream singer here unburdened himself of the harp and sat down, staring moodily into the dull, turbid water. I put my trust, as always, in John, and was prepared to wait. He must know what he was doing, and it was his pilgrimage.

The tall man was not so patient.

"Why do we wait?"

"For the tide," replied the old man. His chin rested on a scarred hand, and the voice seemed muffled by the displaced tangle of his beard.

"Even with the power of the harp, we must pay service to the tide?" asked the last man scornfully, and somewhat bitterly. But he accepted the judgment.

"Play," requested John, "while we wait." Perhaps that was why he still followed the old man. He thought that the secret might still lie in the that which echoed from the singer's mind.

The singer of dreams set the harp between his knees and stretched his fingers over the strings. He brushed them lightly, and they leapt to life, playing their own tune. His many voices joined in, and the sound of the sea died away completely.

I was perched atop a building in a city of silver and glass. Huge towers, spires and minarets stood high, joined together by sweeping silver filaments, burning and throbbing in the noon sunlight. It was the old sun; the bright yellow sun. The square below was embellished with crystal statues, and in its center was a glassy pool. The ground was like a flowing transparency of blue glass. The peaks of tall skyscrapers gleamed and flashed brilliantly like multifaceted gems. And everywhere, there was light. There were no dark, shadowy corners, for this city cast a light of its own.

John's dream, this. That was obvious. His old dream—the dream he still harbored somewhere in his mind. The Great Ages. The Age of Man's Conquests.

On one of the nearby skyscrapers, four humans stood on a balcony looking up at the luminous blue sky. They were richly dressed with flowing white and purple robes, with golden bracelets and lace collars. Their feet were encased in crystalline sandals, and their legs were covered by iridescent silky cloth. They were highly ornamented and bejewelled. The one female in the party wore large diamond earrings and circlets of amethyst, ruby, and zircon round her fingers. On her head, she wore a flashing diamond tiara.

The men also wore rings of polished precious stone, but had coronets of helically twisted silver and gold. Around their necks hung opalescent chains of fire. Their strong, slender hands gripped the protective rail tightly as they leaned backwards over the balcony to stare upwards. Their features were uniformly handsome and well tanned. Their eyes were bright and glowed like their gems, their lips full and red like rubies. Their brows were heavily arched and dark. Their hair was as black as ebony—the men's trimmed to the shoulder, the woman's long and hanging down her back in shining tresses. Each countenance was fresh and alive.

Oh John, I thought, *why must your dream be so impossible? Couldn't there be an age of triumph without this decoration and outrageous perfection? It's too shallow, John, too far away.*

A sudden flock of dark birds shot across the sky and disappeared behind the buildings. A tiny, silver-shiny aeroplane crossed my field of mental vision. A small, black shape was slowly descending. My eyes adjusted to the distance, and I saw a large winged creature spiraling slowly down towards the city, almost directly above the building on whose roof we stood. At first glimpse it appeared to be a huge bird, but I soon realized that it had the form of a winged man, like Raon the Outcast of the city of night. For a moment, I thought that it might be Raon—that John was building new encounters into old dreams. But it wasn't—he was too heavily built.

He flew upright, his arms folded against his chest as he drifted down like an autumn leaf. His eyes had picked out something in the city below, and he seemed to be looking straight at me. I wondered whether I was as visible to him as he to me.

Up in the dazzling sky, far above the descending birdman, I saw a second black dot weaving purposefully above the needle-spired towers.

At the same moment, the four watchers became aware of me, apparently by following the direction of the birdman's gaze. I was visible—a small, shabby figure on top of a building in a perfect city. I must have looked supremely strange, in my travel-stained clothes. Or was that what they saw? I could not be sure. Perhaps they saw all four of us. They seemed excited for a second, then turned their gaze back to the sky, beginning to show signs of agitation.

The higher black dot sank low enough to be defined as a second winged man, who circled and then hovered for a moment in direct line with my own position and the first fly-

ing man. The latter flapped languidly toward me, as if to in-
spect whatever strange sight assailed his eyes at closer range.

I saw the wholly naked body, the thin, weak legs with
three toes to each foot, the hands with the slender, tapering
fingers and the powerfully muscled arms. I saw the projec-
tions fused into the shoulder blades where the large, sleek-
feathered wings extended from the body, and the fantastic-
ally developed muscles of the man's torso and the base of his
spine.

The second birdman folded his wings so that the alulae
met and the primaries were inclined horizontal to his body,
and he plummeted like a stone.

The hovering man watched me with a puzzled expression on his face. He had dark, narrow eyes which gleamed
with curiosity, and tiny folds of skin that puckered across his
forehead. His wings were spread wide, curved to support him
as they beat softly and rhythmically.

The four on the balcony below stared in fascination,
eyes glimmering with emotion.

I wanted to shout a warning, but I had no voice.

The second wingman arrived. His wings shot out to
brake his fall, then began to beat furiously as he swept
across, just above the first. His fingers, which I saw suddenly
to be equipped with artificial steel claws, raked the hoverer's
back.

The smitten man's head shot back and up as his mighty
back muscles contracted. And as the hunter soared round, his
razor talons flashed and slit the bared throat to parallel
streamers of red. Bright, frothy arterial blood spouted from
the neck. The dead man's limbs twitched, and he dropped.
The other completed his maneuver with a downward swoop
to catch his victim dexterously beneath the armpits. Then,
flapping even more rapidly, he began to fly slowly down,
bathed in the red blood which sprayed over him, to the four
waiting falconers.

And it was over.

There was a long silence as the waves lapped closer and
closer. I could dangle my fingers in the water as I lay on the
ledge. I tried to see what lay beneath the surface, but the
light was poor and the water thick and oily.

John sat down beside me.

"I thought it was your dream, at first," I said.

"So did I," he replied. His lips were puckered, as though there was a sour taste in his mouth.

The old man was stirring slowly from his trance. I knelt, and helped him to his feet. He supported himself on the harp, and pulled it clear of a reaching wave. Then, saying nothing, he began to play again. He played slowly and quietly, with long rise and fall, but here and there a seeming crescendo which would be overcome by the sheer mass of the rhythm and fade again with its fullness.

It was the sea, I realized abruptly. He was playing to the sea. And so it seemed, for the water abandoned its rippling in the wind. and began to move in accordance with the music. I had known that the music of the harp could bend nature, but I had not been so close before. And the *sea*—the sea was vast and gray and brooding. The dream singer was so tiny and so fragile.

The waters rose to his call as though he was taking over the surging tide from the restless pull of the moon. The power, I realized, was already there. He was merely using it.

The water rose in a great cylinder far above us, now black in the moonlit night. And in the great black tower then appeared a door—a cavern of air leading into the colossus that was held by the harp.

The dream singer inclined his head towards this hole, but the tall man was afraid, and shook his head. John immediately rose and stepped from the ledge into the threshold. I gasped, and tried to pull him back, but he was out of reach, stepping some way within the gaping maw of the tunnel. He stood still, and it might have been a staircase hewn in stone, for it supported him easily.

The dark man, reassured, followed him, and I plunged after—not because I wanted to go, but because I would not leave my brother. I was swept by overwhelming terror, but nothing happened. The dream singer left the harp and followed me. I expected the tower to collapse and crush us all, but the harp played on.

The three of us *descended*. We went down into the bowels of the ocean, ignoring the heights of the column.

Our footing was easy. It mattered not whether we trod on the smooth face of water or on emptiness, for at times the tunnel was vertical. We were held still, in perfect balance, by the music of the harp.

The journey was a long one. My feet traced out the path automatically. There was no light, but I knew that the other three were mere feet away.

Then, "We are here," stated the dream singer.

Suddenly, there was light, blinding light, in such profusion that I was bent double by its searing agony. There was a wild cry which must have come from the tall man, for it was not John's voice.

There were other sounds too—a whispering and a tantalizing susurration like the calling of a faraway voice. There was a soft laughter which I knew belonged to the dream singer, and the singing of a tiny bell.

I willed my eyes to open so that I could see the source of these voices, but they would not. The blast of light had sealed them shut, and they remained so to protect my delicate retinas.

Then there was a sound like the rushing of a storm wind, and my body was snatched like a dry leaf and whirled upward. At first, I thought the water had folded up. but then I caught the strains of the ocean music of the harp—now fast, almost frenzied. In my violent upsurge I was thrust against another body. Merely the feel of flesh and clothing, but enough to assure me I was not alone.

Somehow, I contrived to catch an edge of the clothing and cling tight. I believed it to be John, but I could not know for certain.

The upward fall eased, and finally, as we were vomited from the funnel, we rolled only gently with the abatement of motion, and did not hurt ourselves as we came to rest on the black, hard rock.

I relinquished my hold on the cloak I had grasped, and was astonished to find that it belonged neither to the dream singer nor to John, but to the dark man.

The dream singer, some feet away, seemed to be soothing the harp strings into quietude as the ocean relapsed into its natural state. He picked up the harp and set off along the ledge. The dark man, without speaking, walked away in the other direction.

I made to follow the white-haired old man, but John restrained me. "There's no more need," he said.

"You've seen what you wanted to see?" I asked him. "The dream you thought was yours?"

"Yes."

"And?"

"Perhaps none of us owns our dreams."

"What now?"

"The pilgrimage. We must find what we seek. I don't know that we have a great deal of time left."

"Time?"

"I'm ill, Matthew."

Silence, while I stared at him. It wasn't possible. Xavier had been older than Joaz; Joaz older than I. But John had thirteen years in hand of me. He couldn't die. He was so young.

"What happened, down there?" I asked him, thinking that he must have been hurt.

"The last man decided that he didn't want to die just yet."

"Why did he ever want to?"

John's eyes searched out and held my own. "Because he was lonely, I suppose."

I shook my head.

"We must move," said John. "We must find what we seek."

"You can't die," I said. *You can't leave me alone*, is what I meant.

I needed him. He was everything I had. I didn't need the safety of my home world. I didn't need the contentment I'd carried with me ever since my dream died. I only needed him.

Don't leave me here!

XXIV.

THE END OF TIME

We see chaos within chaos.

We see the fury of irrationality.

We see Earth, Air, Fire and Water take arms against one another and tear the world apart in the wake of their combat.

Beneath us, and all around us, the surface splits, showing faces of rock for a bare instant, and then slams together again. Fountains of molten rock and flame leap to the skies, dying like roman candles in a lunatic tumble of sparks.

A green pulp of vegetation is visible in places, and in others signs of its passing can be seen in black ashes. The animals bound to land would have been the first to perish. The birds might possibly be the last. I can see, high in the sky, tiny black specks that might be birds. There they might stay, temporarily safe above the turmoil until terror or hunger or fatigue consumes them, and they fall to their deaths. Behind their slowly drifting silhouettes, the sun watches, aloof and uncaring. And red. Brick red.

The plain ripples like a flag in the wind under the straining forces of the earthquake. Great cracks appear in the rolling ground, and large islands of rock slip down into the jaws of the Earth with a shudder, whole new lands rise up on tides of tremendous force. Large boulders vibrate and are stirred into motion. Vast clouds of dust begin to rise, carrying with them the spores which are the most likely hope—indeed the only hope—of life's regaining a foothold on this fevered land.

163

Slivers of rock and soil slide from the edges of widening cracks, like great rivers of dust, to fill the yawning crevasses. A blister of rock bursts somewhere beneath our lonely station atop a quiet hill, and the base of the mount is bathed in flame and lava. For a long instant, the stream of destruction surrounds us, and the clawing fingers of its heat reach up to tear at our skins and rob us momentarily of clear vision. But the smoke dies, and the heat is snatched away by a great wind, and we may watch again as the Earth vomits its unknown sickness into the painted sky.

Travelling from the far end of a new-formed furrow in the ground, a vast wave of earth and rock is swept by molten lava to fill the new valley. A second wave sets out from the nearer mouth, each travelling with fearful velocity to a powerful impact that will shake the world. Large rocks are hurled from the crest of each lava wave as they speed to their mutual destruction. The edges course ahead and the wavefronts become concave. The vast faces become steeper and steeper as the valley is rent beneath them.

Then they meet, in a bewildering gout of colored flame. We watch a chain of mountains on the horizon explode, see their anger hurled defiantly at the unreachable sun. A fissure splits the plain apart to the left of us, and the lava begins to pour over the edge and drop to its sightless depths. The edges of the fissure crumble, and the gaping abyss is sealed again.

Vivid lightning dissects the darkening horizon. Pinnacles and spires of granite topple. We see in the sky the wrathful reflection of a vast fire, sweeping ever on towards us, expanding to either side. We see the flames themselves as they cavort above the bursting wounds in the Earth's crust. We see the plumes and vortices of cyclonic smoke, red in the castellate flames.

And the mighty wind, attendant upon the firestorm, plucks us from our coign of vantage and hurls us from the dying earth, so that we might not see the quiet that must follow, when the spores in the dust clouds will settle back to the surface, to begin again.

* * * * * * *

"It's too late," he says.

"What do you mean?"

"I'm not strong enough, Matthew."

"I'll carry you."

"It wouldn't do any good."

"It must."

"It's over Matthew. I'm dying."

"No."

"Like Xavier. Like Joaz."

"No." I am crying.

"You're the only one now, Matthew."

"I can't be alone."

"You must go on. You must see what we came to see."

"Don't leave me, John."

"I'm dying, Matthew."

"Not yet. Please, not yet."

* * * * * * *

Bloated as a blister and black-blue as a bruise it lies, in a creamy white froth on the encrusted ground. I feel an overwhelming sensation of revulsion as I watch it flopping slowly about on its rotting cushion.

Its arms, like swollen slime-threads, radiate from its body to dangle in matted festoons in the stagnant water of a nearby pool. They are covered with warts of vivid sky blue and dotted with purple suckers. I cannot count them, they are so many. It reminds me somewhat of a jellyfish or a feather-star.

Oily liquid exudes from lilac pores of its surface and drips to the ground beneath its belly.

On top of the body, there is an eye. I can just make out the thin, iridescent blue of the translucent lens which is set in a platelike iris of many colors. The eye has two lids, violet-black in color, and a thin nictitating membrane, which flips back and forth at metronomically regular intervals.

The animal—if it is an animal—lies with its single massive eyeball turned to an equally empty sky. It has no visible mouth, and no other appendages save for the gelatinous coils that I have called arms.

It is neither ferocious nor, I suppose, dangerous, yet I think of it as terrible and frightening. I wonder whether this thing was actually born on the Earth or whether it might not be a visitor from some distant, loathsome world whose children all look like this.

The hideous creature is completely out of keeping with its surroundings. There is grass and soil, sand and sky, sun and clouds, water and wind, flowers and flies, trees and clay, birds and bushes.

I think it might be dead, and that its slow, rhythmic motion might be caused by some regular natural impulse. But it heaves, once, in a soundless, squelching sigh like a corpulent bag of fetid air.

And we run away.

* * * * * * *

"I'm dying, Matthew."

"Don't die, child. I need you. There'll be no one left to carry out this crazy quest of yours. I can't do it. I know you want me to, but it's no good. I'm no dreamer. No believer. You know I have no faith. If you die, John, you've failed, no matter what I might do. There's no need to die. You mustn't fail. I'll carry you forever. You can sleep. I'll give you food. There's nothing can touch you. Nothing to harm you. I'll look after you. It has to be you, John. You're the one with the mission. You're the one with the soul. You're the Firefly who casts his own light. There's no light in the world now, John, if you leave it. The last man's dead. There's only you, John. I'm nothing. Only you. You won't die, John, not without *knowing.* Will you?"

"I *do* know, Matthew. I have faith."

* * * * * * *

Ash all around us. We are surrounded by a flaky mass of it, forming a jet black desert which stretches to the edge of the lava-encrusted hills. It floats in the air in a thousand large paper wisps, a million small slivers and particles, a billion dusty fragments which the wind gently stirs into an eddying, boiling cloud. It settles like feathery gray down. It rises languidly, like smoke.

Night-black rocks present scoured surfaces to our eyes, splitting the blackness up into grotesque angular shadows. It is black dark and the full, cold moonlight glances lightly down to shy away from the harsh surfaces, hardly daring to touch them.

In the half-light, the stones assume the shapes of deformed dwarfs, crouching giants, weird chimeras, fallen towers and twisted trees.

It is a cold, crisp, strange world, yet the stars are the same stars that I have always known. At least, I think so.

* * * * * * *

"Lay me down, now, Matthew."
"It's not much further."
"Where?"
I stop. Where indeed?

* * * * * * *

The sun rises over the sea. It is deep-red beyond the dust-laden air.

The dull, turbid ocean washes sluggishly up the beach, smoothing out the slightly-stirred gray sand. There are no shells on the beach, no seaweed. It is bare, expansive, gray piebald with brown. It stinks.

Inland, the vegetation is poor. Squat, loose grass spaces drooping shrubs for a hundred yards between the beach and a complex of shattered rock and screeslope, where one or two trees grow, and several flowers hang on to slight patches of soil.

Within the rocks, in the very center of the island, is a basin three miles in diameter—a well filled with thick tropical vegetation—a profusion of lush green and thick stalks.

There is no one alive.

* * * * * * *

I lay him down, and shield him from the wind. Red sand blows in my eyes, but I keep his face between my arms, protected.

"I can't go on," I say. "Not me."

"You must."

"It's you who know all the answers. Not I. I don't understand. I don't know what to feel if I see it. I don't know *why*."

"But they always were *your* dreams, Matthew. I only borrowed them. You can have them back, now."

I remember the desert, where we flee beneath the stars, while the wolves howl and follow us, and the winds whisper to me of death and despair. The sand whines across the bare rock, pursued by the cloudless storm, and we follow its trail, ourselves pursued and driven. The night is clean and ugly, moving its clumsy hands, the winds, in a cruel and relentless fashion, which hurts us and tells me of my loneliness.

Always we hear the wolves cry, the sound thrown at us by the wind. Sometimes they seem to sob, often they laugh in mocking delight. We would see them as they dance across the face of the moon, but they creep in gullies and will not show themselves. Like worms they crawl and slither in the slashes which cut and ribbon the desert floor.

We cannot stop, although I doubt that it is courage or strength which drives us on. Nor is it fear or desperation. Madness holds us like the night holds the desert, with no escape and no hope.

He might see, as I do, the madness that makes the desert flow past us and echo the howling of wolves deep inside our skulls. He might see the black shadows cloaking the land burying us in comforting oblivion. He cannot see me—this I know. He never knew me at all.

A long time afterwards, someone reaches out and touches me. It is the singer of dreams.

"You," I say. "Only you. It's empty, but for you."

"Is he dead?" asks the old man. His violet eyes look slantwise down at the body.

"Of course he's dead. There's only one left now, and that's only me. What can I do?"

"What do you want to do?"

"He says to go on."

"And will you?"

"What's the point?"

But I know the answer to that. There is no point. There is nobody left to provide reasons. I am alone. Alone with my non-belief, non-truth, non-existence. It is the first time that I have been alone since I lost my own dreams, in a garden long ago.

"I loved him," I say, as if the singer of dreams could ever have doubted it.

"He was my brother," I explain.

The dream singer begins to play. I think it is a hymn, or a deathsong. But it isn't. His body is splitting and decaying, as if cold flame is burning it away. As if all the time that ever was is taking him apart.

And he is growing.

XXV.

THE WORLDS BEYOND THE WORLD

What is happening?

A puzzle. A jigsaw puzzle with words for pieces.

Álvaro. *We* cannot know, for even if we see the After-man, we could not understand him...to conquer, don't you see, you have to make something *yours*...you have to make it a part of you...something you can control and direct...the Afterman must be a step beyond, in that he must be *removed* entirely from the influence of the environment. He will be *free.*

A dream. I'm not John. I'm Matthew.... I'm Matthew, not John....

The man who walked through time. We were reptiles once, your ancestors and mine...common men will go on and on and on, but they'll be the apes and monkeys of the future...just animals, with no purpose and no destiny.

A dream. Kindly shut the door. Notice that EXIT is on the inside. *You cannot leave this way.*

John. That *one* of us sees—that is enough for all...we will be carrying the hopes and the blessings of hundreds of men—thousands more in the past and in the future... If one of us can see, if *one* of us can *know* the emergence and triumph of the Afterman, then that will be enough.... We'll go together...to the end of time.... You and I will both see the Afterman...I *know* it.

A dream. A garden, where there were golden fountains...I had come to find something I had forgotten...to seek something new as well...I had come to bury my regrets...I asked for hope...she was dead...SHE WAS DEAD!

Myself. I saw the world as a god might have seen it, but I was no god...what I saw *meant* something, for all that I could see hardly anything at all.... There was something in life that was sedate and calm...an unruffled conqueror moving with self-assured strategy.... I came to know intimately the philosophy of life.

John. You're not alone.... There's nothing new.... But they always were your dreams, Matthew.... I only borrowed them.... You can have them back, now.

* * * * * * *

Evolution works with the *young*. Not with the old, the mature, the defined, but with the plastic and the changeable—that which has yet to develop. A man is a man, but the gastrula that becomes a man might, with such a subtle change, become something else entirely. An imago, an adult, is a complete being. It has not the capacity for further change. A chicken is only *one way* by which an egg may make another egg. The egg has the choice. The chicken does not.

Evolution works with the *larvae*, the maggots and the medusae and the nymphs and the tadpoles.

That is the secret.

Metamorphosis.

* * * * * * *

The singer of dreams. It is all of me. My knowledge, my memories, my many shapes and my emotions. It is my every thought expressed as a single unit, my every dream fulfilled. It is the limit of my creation...

How could you know? How could you know that there was another creation yet to come? Does a caterpillar know that it will become a butterfly? Does a nymph know that it will be a lacewing for a single day before it dies?

You *are* the Afterman, but even *you* did not know.

171

* * * * * * *

There is a voice in my mind.

"Imagine a pool of water. It is raining. Every minute, hundreds of ripples are formed. They expand and cross each other. But they do not bar each other's progress. Each individual ripple pursues its own course outward across the pool, but at every moment, hundreds of others are touching it.

"The universes are ripples, their circumferences are change. As a ripple expands, it touches others, and time grows in extent, but not linearly. Where the universes meet, there is no disruption of their course. But each intersection is a focus for multiplex perception.

"I don't understand."

Could a reptile understand a man...?

* * * * * * *

I feel myself torn from the imploding swathes of darkness, wrenched apart and dissipated in the windless night. The restraining prison of my body is discarded, the concealed spaces of my mind erupt outwards into the void. And I grow, expanding like a hurricane, like a shockwave. Like a billowing fireball I expand in an orgasm of self-consuming energy. The empty shell of my universe is cracked open and cast off, the clutches of its mode of existence totally forgotten My existence as a sub-universal being is shattered and left to the ravenous waves, which bear me outwards and onwards, growing and ever growing until my *mind* reaches away from the tiny tippling spheres to embrace my new macrocosm.

The darkness is filled with haloes, multitudinous universes welded into exquisitely thin rings by their evolution, in tilting rotation and gyration. Their starsprinkle glisters in the black night, transforming the spinning rings into Catherine wheels. They converge and draw apart, blend and divide, clash and interlace, simultaneously and eons apart, spinning joyously in their own gaudy light.

And still I grow.

Now I see a shadow, a shadow cast on darkness by darkness. It signifies power and austerity. In this existence without dimensions it seems far above me, below me, around, beyond and within me.

Suddenly, the spiraling circles are within me, vibrating with my formless expansion. I pulse with the multiple universes and they are one with my soulbeat. They pulse faster and more brightly, their innumerable sparks bursting into individual instants of ephemeral glory and light, only to fade in the same instant, a million transitory sparks which flash and die.

And now I am *one* with this greater existence, *one* with each universe and *one* with Infinity. I am the absolute and the eternal. Time goes out like a snuffed candle and the universes are immaterial.

The great shadow bursts in again on my inhuman mind. Like a hot vapor, I rush to fill the whole of my existence. My mind knows all I have seen, and remembers all that I will see.

Like a rising sun, I come.

Like a firefly.

And boldly, I cry to the timelessness, to the shadow, and to all: "I AM!"

* * * * * * *

John's body is still cradled in my arms. There is empty desert all around us. I am dying. I must, for I cannot live alone and there is nothing else left. But I have seen the triumph of the Afterman. I have seen what John came to see, which John knew only through his faith. But is it enough?

Am I Matthew, and not John? As I hold his head in my arms, I am still trying to ask *why*?

I wish I had a dream, to keep me company.

AUTHOR'S NOTE

This novel is based on a series of fragments written between 1964 and 1966; ten (including some by Craig Mackintosh) were patched up in April 1965 to form a novelette called "Beyond Time's Aegis," which was published in the November 1965 issue of *Science-Fantasy* under the pseudonym "Brian Craig." It was my first sale, and the one which convinced me—despite the evidence of much subsequent failure—that it was worth continuing to write. The novelette was rewritten and the second part patched together as a continuation in January and February of 1971; I had sold five novels by then, but had failed to sell two more, and felt that I had lost all creative impetus. The revision was not a serious attempt to produce something salable; I suppose it was an eccentric exercise in personal reappraisal.

Now, at over forty years of age, I have succeeded in erasing almost entirely the memories of my miserable teenage years, which proved too embarrassing and humiliating to be tolerable. One of the few I have held on to is a memory of sitting in the ground floor lab of the Old Rectory, in the grounds of Manchester Grammar School, during a zoology class. Francis Minns was making one of his ever-heroic attempts to dramatize the wisdom that he was trying to impart to mostly-uncaring ears.

"The cells in your body," he said, "are constantly being replaced. In eight years, the noses on your faces will not be the ones which are there now, although you will not have noticed the change."

I already knew—by virtue of having read a science fiction story which cited it—that the kind of process to which my teacher referred had earlier been dramatized as "the paradox of Achilles' ship."

It is true. We are constantly being remade, molecule by molecule, cell by cell, memory by memory, understanding by understanding; the continuity of our personal history is an illusion. The person who carried out the 1971 revision of this material was not the same person who wrote the original fragments, although he still felt an intimate connection with the old person; that is presumably why Matthew (who did not exist prior to the revision process) is so closely and perversely akin to the "Firefly" who was the protagonist of "Beyond Time's Aegis." The person who wrote this "Author's Note" in 1992 is so far removed from either of them as to find this book utterly strange and alien. It does not come remotely close to making sense, and exhibits certain tendencies of which the present author thoroughly disapproves. Nevertheless, it retains—for the present author, at least—a certain naive charm and psychological fascination. The ridiculous, incompetent, and introverted child who wrote the bits of this book, and the alienated, incompetent, bitter young man who patched the bits together, both wanted to write something different from anything that had ever been written before. Through the process of writing, they wanted to transport themselves away from the horrific awkwardness of their everyday existence; to go "anywhere out of the world," the further the better. They wanted to write, to produce, and to experience something deep and strange and comforting. I still try, time and time again, after my own more calculated and hopefully more effective fashion, to do the same thing.

—Brian Stableford
Reading, Berkshire, England
9 December 1992